Secret Diaries:
Confessions of a Submissive

Claire Thompson

ISBN: 1-4392-3740-9
ISBN-13: 9781439237403

To order additional copies, please contact us.
BookSurge
www.booksurge.com
1-866-308-6235
orders@booksurge.com

chapter I

TESS MIGHT NOT have noticed the small trunk, more of a strongbox really, but something about it caught her eye. Underneath the dust, it was silver. Aluminum, in fact, and sturdily built. Pushing aside the piles of junk, she scooted over to the trunk. The clasp was locked with a small but sturdy padlock. She pulled at it, but it didn't give.

Tess had been especially close with her grandmother and had thought she knew everything there was to know about her grandmother. So what was this locked box?

The ringing phone downstairs drew her away.

"Winston residence," she said, slightly out of breath.

"Olivia." The voice was deep and resonant.

"Excuse me, who's calling?"

"Forgive me, I thought you were Olivia. Is she available, please?"

"Oh, dear," Tess's voice wavered, hating to impart the news to someone who obviously didn't know. "Who is this, please?"

The man hesitated but finally offered, "This is James Stevenson. An old friend. I'm afraid I've been out of the country for some months. Is Olivia all right?"

"I'm sorry, Mr. Stevenson, to be the bearer of bad news, but my grandmother passed away last month." Tears sprang to Tess's eyes, and she tried to keep her voice steady as she spoke to the stranger, who might now be dealing with his own grief.

"Oh," the man said, in a sudden exhale of breath. I'm sorry," he began, his voice suddenly cracking. "Thank you for...for letting me know." Tess heard the click of his receiver and she gently cradled her own.

She sat thinking for a while, trying to place the man's name. James Stevenson. *An old friend.* Clearly he'd very affected by the news and yet he'd hung up so abruptly.

Tess's eyes filled with tears for the hundredth time that weekend, as her gaze fell on a photograph of Nana and Pop. It was from early in their marriage, sometime in the fifties. The picture was black and white, but by the shading and light, one could see that Nana had fair hair and skin. She was smiling, the big happy smile of someone young and in love. Her face was turned toward her husband, who stared directly at the camera, his expression self-conscious and stiff as he posed for the lens.

Olivia, though, seemed unaware of the camera. Her hair was pulled back in a careless ponytail, tendrils of unruly hair blowing gently against her cheek. Her face looked fresh and open. A Kansas farm girl kind of freshness, with a sprinkling of freckles across her broad, snubbed nose.

Tess held the framed photo, one she'd looked at many times before, and mentally compared herself with the woman she saw there. Nana was younger even than Tess's twenty-five years in the old picture. Where Olivia was blonde and freckled, Tess had her father's dark brown hair and hazel eyes that changed from green to gray depending on her outfit or her mood. Tess's was a more delicate face, with high, fine cheekbones and eyes almost too large for her face. She had always envied her Nana's open, sunny good looks.

Next to the photo were several large seashells, their horny exteriors protecting the delicate, milky pink curves inside. Tess lifted a nautilus shell, cradling it gently in her hands. It brought back sharp memories of summers spent collecting shells at dawn, while everyone but she and Nana slept. The world had seemed to belong only to the two of them then.

Tess sighed loudly, wiping a tear from her cheek with the back of her hand. Everything about this old house was steeped in memories of Nana and Pop. She needed to get the hell out of there and home to her little cat, Butterscotch.

Yet she found her mind drifting back to the strongbox in the attic. What was in there that it had to be kept locked? And where was the key? Tess remembered she had seen a ring of keys in the desk when she was going through old papers.

Hurrying over to the desk, she pulled open the drawers, trying to remember where she'd seen those keys. Ah! There they were, hidden behind a container of pushpins and paper clips. She pulled out the old key ring and examined the keys on it. There was a small key that looked like it might fit the padlock.

Returning to the attic, she knelt in front of the silver strongbox and fit the key into the lock. It wouldn't budge.

She saw that it wasn't the right key after all. None of the other keys on the ring were even close.

She gave up and went downstairs, closing the blinds and leaving the house with several boxes in tow. The strongbox would have to wait, as Butterscotch would be hungry.

_*_

Monday after work found Tess back at her grandmother's house. She might not have come back so soon, but that mysterious strongbox had been on her mind. Who knew what was in it? Maybe jewels and gold doubloons! She laughed to herself at the thought. That was just what Nana would have guessed, and she would have actually been crestfallen when it only turned out to be old newspapers and magazines.

Which was probably what was in there—junk. Maybe a stack of old S&H green stamps booklets, filled and waiting to be mailed for a free sewing machine. Or love letters exchanged between Nana and Pop while they were still courting. Though Tess couldn't imagine Pop ever writing a love letter. Still, her curiosity was piqued.

Whose box was it? Nana's or Pop's? She thought it must be Nana's, as Pop had kept everything of value to him in the shed off the garage. That had been his domain, full of fishing tackle, gardening implements and girlie magazines he thought no one knew he had.

Pop rarely went into the attic. He couldn't stand the clutter, he said, and left it to Livvie to deal with. So, it must be Nana's. And yet, it was locked, even though Pop never went up there. What was so important that she had to lock it?

Today Tess was armed with a bolt cutter in the event that a final search did not yield a key. She looked again in all the drawers and especially in the night table on Nana's side of the bed but no luck. Slowly she climbed the attic stairs, trying to think where Nana might have hidden that key.

Suddenly, Tess remembered when they used to stay with Nana and Pop at their summer beach cottage and Nana would remind her, "The key's on the window ledge, dear. Up high. If we're down at the shore when you get here, just let yourself in."

The window ledge. There were two windows in the attic. Tess went over to one of them and felt along the top of the window. Nothing. She put her fingers along the second ledge and something scuttled away, causing her to jerk her hand away and let out an involuntary squeal.

Recovering herself, she put her hand again up to the dusty ledge and slowly moved her fingers along it until they bumped against something flat and cold to the touch. It was a key! She closed her fingers around with a satisfied smile. Nana would have been proud of her detective work.

Quickly she walked over to the strongbox, pausing for a moment, wondering if she had the right now that Nana was dead to open it. Did Nana's right to privacy disappear when she died?

Tess wavered for a second, debating if she should ask her mother's opinion. But her curiosity won out. It wasn't like she would do anything to compromise Nana's privacy.

Putting any misgivings to rest, she pushed the key into the lock. It turned smoothly with a satisfying click, and slowly she opened the lid.

No doubloons. No priceless gold trinkets or ancient documents worth millions. There were just some old notebooks. These were worth locking up? They looked dusty and faded, like they hadn't been written in or looked at for quite a while. They were thin, with pale blue covers, like composition notebooks for a final exam. Old account ledgers? She lifted the top one and opened it to the first page.

Sitting back, she realized she had stumbled upon someone's diary. Someone's very private diary. Across the inside of the cover was written the word "FIVE". There were only five altogether, and she saw that each one had a number inscribed on the inner cover. She looked until she found number "ONE" and sat back with it.

Recognizing her grandmother's neat flowing handwriting, Tess began to read.

~*~

October 11, 1961

Mr. Stevenson said that I should write here. He said it would help me to sort out my thoughts. He told me to get myself a little notebook and keep it here at work somewhere safe.

I'm not sure where to start. When I asked Mr. Stevenson where he thought I should, he said, in that deep voice of his, "Start at the beginning. And be honest. Explore your feelings and don't censor yourself. No one but you will read your private thoughts."

"Not even you?" I asked him.

"Most especially not me."

I believe him. I think it would go against his grain to lie.

Well, I shall start at the beginning, as Mr. Stevenson instructed.

Mr. James Stevenson is an attorney, and I am his secretary. I can't believe Frank let me go back to work, but since Jeannie is in second grade already, and I'm so bored at home, he said it was all right. Plus, I know the extra money will help with our summer vacations! I've already saved up some since I started here in early September.

~*~

James Stevenson! The man who had called! Of course, Tess remembered now. Nana had worked in an attorney's office, and that was his name. She had worked there for many years, and obviously they had remained in touch since her retirement. Just what was their relationship now? Tess was confused, and not a little intrigued.

The detective in her began to piece some of the puzzle together. Calculating in her head, she said aloud, "Let's see—" squinting up at the ceiling, "—1961, so Nana must have been twenty-nine."

Why in the world would her boss instruct her to keep a diary? Well, the evidence was before her, and so Tess read on.

~*~

October 11, 1961, continued

Mr. Stevenson is a very exacting man, and he insists on perfection. He reminds me time and again that an attorney can't afford to make mistakes, and therefore neither can his secretary. The first time he whacked my hand with the ruler, I have to admit I was surprised, but I'm coming to see that it is indeed effective. My typing has improved markedly.

~*~

What the hell was this? Tess looked at it again to make sure she hadn't misread. Whacking her hand with a ruler? This was no ordinary office situation, even if it was way back in 1961!

Tess shifted. She was uncomfortable sitting there on the dusty floor of the attic. Scooping up the pile of notebooks, she went downstairs. She made herself a cup of tea, prolonging the moment when she returned to the bizarre diaries.

For the first time, her comfortable, confident knowledge of who and what her grandmother had been was being shaken. She considered for a moment tossing all the diaries and forgetting she had ever seen them. But even as she thought this, she dismissed it. There was no way she was going to throw these out. As upsetting as it might be, she was going to read these things from beginning to end. She had to know.

Sitting down at Nana's old Formica table, Tess sipped her cinnamon tea and lifted number "ONE" again. Now she read steadily, her eyes wide, her mouth falling open.

~*~

October 13, 1961
I can't believe he used the ruler on my bottom yesterday! Especially just for a silly thing like a run in my stock-

ing. I'm sure the client didn't see it, either. I can't even believe I'm sitting here writing this, but Mr. Stevenson has given me an extra-long lunch hour, and he told me to use it wisely. I know he wants me to write. Probably afraid if I don't get it out here, I'll tell Frank my employer smacked my rear with a ruler!

How did all this happen? When did my boss become this bizarre disciplinarian? It's been six weeks now since I've been here. At first, Mr. Stevenson was just your normal everyday old boss. Well, maybe not "everyday" as he's always been a stickler for perfection, right from the beginning.

Distinguished-looking and very much the proper attorney. He's thirty-four, I know because I saw his birth date on some of his certification records. He's married and has two sons. His last secretary was named Millicent Willis, she quit this past year when she married, and so he needed someone new.

Thinking back, the interview *was* rather unusual, but I guess I was so eager for the job that I brushed it aside. I remember now how he went on and on about how exacting he was, and how he'd grown used to Miss Willis' 120 word-per-minute dictation. I don't believe that—I do 105 and I'm very fast. I remember he went on about her ability to proof a legal document and catch every single teeny-tiny error. He said if he hired me, I'd be on probation for six weeks and that I'd be punished for any infraction.

Yes! He actually said punished, and when I raised my eyebrows and said, "Excuse me?" he kind of backtracked, explaining that he only meant he was very exacting and wouldn't tolerate incompetence. In short, I'd either be up to his high standards or out the door.

But I'm coming to realize you can't be up to Mr. Stevenson's standards. They're impossible. I'd really like to meet this Miss Willis. She must be a saint here on this earth, with her perfect skills and perfect everything else. Makes me want to slap her!

What is it about Mr. Stevenson that makes me want to please him so?

Partly, it's that voice. Sonorous. That's the word that comes to mind. It's pleasing, but more than that, it's commanding. Lulling, lilting, moving. I feel like I'm tethered to him on some secret level and his voice draws me to him. One wants to immediately obey whatever he asks. One wants, almost desperately, to please.

His voice haunts me. I dream of it. But the things he expects? These bizarre little punishments! Why do I tolerate the smack of his ruler and his relentless critiquing of my apparently numerous failings?

What in God's name is wrong with me?

_*_

October 17, 1961
Yesterday, I told Mr. Stevenson that I quit. He said he wouldn't accept the resignation. I said, "Why ever not? I obviously don't measure up to Miss Magnificent Willis."

"Come into my office, Olivia," he said, not even looking back to see if I followed. Well, I did follow, waiting to see what he had to say. Frank has already come to rely on my paycheck, and I dreaded telling him I'd quit, but enough is enough.

What precipitated my decision? Well, yesterday morning Mr. Stevenson told me two very important clients were coming in and he wanted to make sure we made an excellent impression, as they could throw a lot more business our way. He actually asked me to bend over so he could inspect the back of my stockings. Given that run last week, he explained, as if it were perfectly natural for a boss to inspect his secretary's legs!

That's part of it—the way he's so confident and sure when he's "disciplining" me. The way he acts as if this were the most natural thing in the world between a boss and his secretary. I find myself blushing and stammering, desperate to please him, chagrined, humiliated even, when I have failed yet again to measure up.

I find myself saying, "I'm sorry, Sir, it won't happen again." And while it's happening, it doesn't occur to me that this is very odd behavior on both our parts! I haven't worked in an office before, it's true, but I'm certain most attorneys don't keep a ruler at the ready to smack their errant secretaries! And probably most girls would have been out the door after the first rap to their knuckles!

Yet here I sit, writing in this thing because he told me to and instead of protesting, I try harder and harder to please Mr. Stevenson. I don't know why exactly. There's something about him. I haven't conveyed it at all here. I haven't really conveyed much of anything yet, I guess, except that I must be stone-cold crazy.

Suffice it to say, there's something about Mr. Stevenson. You just want to please him. Yet, it's so hard! So, when you do succeed in getting that little half-smile of approval, you feel so good and proud.

So yesterday morning when he instructed me to bend over, for some absurd reason I actually complied, bending over the back of my chair so he could see my calves, which were all that showed, of course. Well, he actually lifted the skirt, right up to the garters! Can you imagine! And ran his hands slowly up and down my thighs. Like I was some kind of hussy!

"Mr. Stevenson!" I admonished in a shocked tone, standing up at once as I pushed his hands away.

I know, I know. Before that, I had let this man swat my hand and my leg and even my bottom (over my skirt) with his little ruler, and here I was acting all affronted. Why didn't I quit before? I can't say exactly. But yesterday was the last straw.

So I thought.

I fumed over it all through my lunch hour, which I took at my desk because it was raining and I didn't want to sit in the park like I usually do. He left, as usual, promptly at one o'clock and returned on the dot of two.

God, listen to me, writing to myself and lying! I'm lying to myself right here on this page, as if I were a stranger who is going to read this and judge me. What is wrong with me?

It wasn't that I was so upset by his feeling my thigh.

It was that I was so aroused by it!

There! I've said it. Frank would never touch me like that—not in a million years. Frank is, well, Frank. Boring Frank. Make love to your wife once a week on Fridays, and keep your eyes closed, no doubt thinking about your next fishing trip, and moving just enough to finish before Jack Parr comes on the television.

God. I can't believe I wrote that. I love Frank! I do. But sex. It's so boring. I've read that it can be wonderful, that it can send tingles through you! You know, I'm just realizing as I sit here writing this that that's exactly it! Mr. Stevenson's hand sent tingles through me! I wanted him to keep touching me, to move higher! It was me I was mad at, not him.

Because I'm married, for better or for worse! And Mr. Stevenson made me think, just for a second, mind you, of someone else. In our eleven years of marriage, I've never so much as looked at another man, and now my boss, of all people, is becoming the center of my fantasies!

Well, I had just finished typing my resignation, feeling very proper and formal. And very nervous. I pulled it out of my typewriter and handed it to him as he passed, saying, "I'm sorry, Mr. Stevenson, but you really give me no choice."

That's when he told me to come into his office. "Sit down, please, Olivia." He looked me up and down in that slow deliberate way he has, like the headmaster at an old-fashioned boarding school in England. I almost expected him to sigh and say that now he would have no choice but to call my parents! In fact, he said, "I think your decision is hasty. Let's discuss it."

Well, I sat and I crossed my legs and folded my arms in a way that was meant to convey that I meant business. There was no way he was going to change my mind. So I thought. Then he totally shocked me.

He said, "Olivia, it's been over six weeks now, and I want you to know you are no longer on probation. The overall quality of your work is excellent, but that isn't why

I want to keep you on. There's something else. I think you know what I'm talking about."

"No, Sir, I don't," I snapped. I know I was being snooty but frankly it felt good, because I kept telling myself that after today I wasn't going to have to come in there anymore and be treated like some kind of wayward child. At the same time, I found myself thrilling to his rare words of praise. Excellent work quality! But that "something else"—I pretended to him, and for a split second, to myself, that I had no earthly idea what he meant.

I was lying.

I can admit it here, because nobody but me will ever see this. This is my secret.

I *did* know what he meant. I don't mean I could articulate it. I'm still not sure I can, but there's something. God, it's embarrassing even to write it here, where no one can see it, but I did know what he meant.

When Mr. Stevenson checks my work my heart starts pounding, and I wait on tenterhooks to see what he'll do. Always that ruler, tap, tap, tapping against his thigh while he reads, carefully, looking—hoping?—for an error, a mistake, something out of place, something missing, so he can say, his voice serious, "Olivia, you've made an error. Come here, and I'll show you." Carefully he points it out, that perfectly manicured fingernail glinting against the misspelled word or an incorrect usage. Calmly he'll say, "Olivia, hold out your hand."

Thwack! Oh, it smarts when he hits my hand. I've tried it different ways, palm up, palm down. I think palm up is easier to take, but he must know this too because he'll hit me harder when I offer my palm.

Okay, I'm getting to it. I'm just going to write this and maybe it will help me understand. Mr. Stevenson says sometimes you know a thing, even when you don't know you know it. What he meant, and what I understood but couldn't express, was that I *liked* what he did to me.

There, I wrote it here, and now I'm blushing, even though I'm sitting here all alone. It isn't just his hand on my thigh or that lovely compelling voice or his good looks. It's everything. The ruler, the stern expression, the exacting requirements that always keep me on my toes.

Mr. Stevenson went to lunch, on the stroke of one, just like always. He goes home to lunch with Mrs. Stevenson, I suppose. I've never asked. I would never ask about his personal life and he never asks about mine.

And I'm still sitting here.

He made me admit it out loud. I found myself admitting that I didn't really want to quit and that I needed what he offered. "You need discipline, Olivia," he said, smiling a little. "I sensed that in you the moment we met. You've never been disciplined because you're smart and you're used to getting over because of that. But I can see through it. I know who you are—I know what you are. And I'm going to teach you to understand. Little by little, but trust me, you will learn. I've been very careful with you up until now, testing the waters, you might say.

"But you've forced my hand with this absurd resignation letter." As he spoke, he tore it up! He actually tore it up! "I won't let you go." He stared at me for a moment, his stern expression softening. In an almost gentle tone, he said, "I need you, Olivia. Forgive my presumption, but you need me too. You need what I offer you."

I stared back at him, not giving him a lick of help. But inside, my brain was in a jumble, my gut in a clench. I *did* need what he offered, whatever the hell it was he was offering.

Then he took my breath with his next remark. "You, Olivia, are going to become my submissive. You will belong to me so completely you will never again even contemplate the thought of leaving me. Ever. Do you understand?"

He actually said that. All of it. I remember what people say. Mr. Stevenson says it's a useful quality, as I can recall exact words that were spoken when he has me sit in on some of his meetings, even without consulting my notes.

Submissive.

I looked it up later. It isn't even a noun, but he uses it as if it were. *To submit, "To yield oneself to the authority or will of another. To surrender. To permit oneself to be subjected to something."*

"I have come to value you," he went on and then he told me he was giving me a twenty percent raise, right there on the spot, effective immediately. He said he wasn't trying to buy me off, but that he wanted to demonstrate in some tangible way how much he valued me.

Well, I pretended that that was what swayed me and I don't mind saying that Frank will be pretty happy about it! But in truth, it wasn't the money. It was the way he said he valued me. The sincerity in his voice and how handsome he looked as he said it. And the way he tore up the letter, like some movie with Gregory Peck—he even looks a little like Gregory Peck! It was very dramatic.

Okay, okay, I'm not being totally honest. As usual. It was also the ruler and all that it implies. I like the ruler—the discipline and the thinly veiled sexual overtones. It makes me aroused. And the way he talked about me belonging to him. I'm not even sure what all he meant, but I got a deep little thrill, right down to my toes, when he said it.

God, I can't believe I'm writing this. I must be crazy.

chapter 2

TESS'S TEA WAS cold. She set down the diary and gazed absently at the little sampler Nana had cross-stitched that had hung over the sink in Nana's kitchen for as long as Tess could remember—"Blessed Are Those Who Clean Up". Now that was the Nana Tess knew. Funny, homey, down-to-earth. Not a sexual bone in her body. Who the hell was this other woman, this secretary who had a boss with a ruler? A handsome Gregory Peck boss with very "exacting" standards. It was like the setup for some cheap S&M novel!

And that was 1961, for God's sake! People didn't do stuff like that back then, did they? No online sex chatrooms, no postings on personal sites—*Stern boss seeks submissive secretary. Must take dictation and spankings.*

And yet...And yet, if Tess were honest with herself, as honest as her grandmother was being with herself in her diary, were the feelings expressed there really so foreign? For Tess, like her grandmother, had as yet unexplored submissive feelings of her own. Her secret fantasies of being held down and "taken" by her lover had remained just that—secret. But they were there.

The idea of working for some guy who was into control—while Tess rejected the idea on the surface, her body was responding otherwise. As bizarre as it was, she was turned on by what she was reading, even if it was her old Nana!

Again she marveled, shaking her head. Her grandmother having submissive thoughts and feelings, all those years ago! It didn't seem possible. Yet, here were these journals, written in Nana's neat, precise hand, the blue ink faded on paper yellowed with time.

This Mr. Stevenson...Tess had half a mind to call him back, and demand an explanation. And yet, she was the one reading someone else's most secret thoughts and dreams. This wasn't any of Tess's business. She thought of herself as free and liberated, sexually and otherwise. Why should she expect a different set of behaviors for her grandmother, just because she was older and of another generation?

Don't judge her, Tess warned herself. That was something Nana had often said. "Don't judge someone just because they don't think exactly like you do. Until you've walked in their shoes, you just have no idea." Well, she was obviously speaking from experience, wasn't she?

Tea forgotten, Tess picked up the journal and continued to read.

~*~

October 19, 1961
Frank was delighted about the raise. He's never admitted it, but he didn't think I had what it took to be

a secretary. He seemed to think that the secretary school I attended after high school was just a front while I went after my "MRS" degree. I get the feeling that he never thought I was cut out for much more than changing diapers and making cookies. But money talks, as Frank is fond of saying, and money is telling him now I'm worth something!

Since we had that little talk, Mr. Stevenson has said straight out he's going to "train" me to behave in a way proper to my station—he actually said that! The man is something out of a Dickens' novel. But he was serious, as I was soon to find out. Things have been moving pretty fast. Maybe a little too fast for me.

Wednesday when I brought in his coffee, I spilled a little when I set it down. The saucer slipped and the coffee slopped over the edge so that a little got on his precious walnut desktop. I had to go back to the kitchenette to get a dishtowel and when I returned he was standing behind his chair, holding that ruler. I felt a twinge in my belly. I felt like I was in first grade and had been sent to the principal's office!

"Olivia," he intoned. "Have you any idea what this desk is worth? It's been in my family for generations. I can't have it being ruined by some careless secretary, now can I?"

"No, Sir," I whispered, feeling my breath catch in my throat. He looked so handsome, so stern standing there, tapping the ruler against the top of his chair.

"You've been here long enough," he went on, "to know the rules. But perhaps they need to be spelled out more clearly for you, since you continue to behave in such a cavalier fashion when it comes to precious antiques."

It was just a drop of coffee! I actually blurted that out to him, and his whole countenance darkened.

"First rule, Olivia, is that you don't offer your opinions, unless I ask for them. I am the boss here. You are not. Is that understood?"

"Yes, Sir," I said, looking down. This was crazy! I knew it, and yet it wasn't crazy either. Something about it felt so right—so exciting! Again the tap, tap, tap of that ruler.

"Second rule. From now on, first infraction is ten strokes with the ruler. Either on your knuckles or on your bottom. I should warn you that I won't be using it so lightly anymore. Now that you're in formal training, your punishments will be real. Repeated infractions will receive escalated punishment. Do I make myself clear?"

"Um..." I hesitated.

"Speak plainly, Olivia. Do not say 'um'. You are not a schoolgirl. Do I make myself clear?"

I swallowed. "Well, Mr. Stevenson, not entirely. I mean, are you saying that you plan to, um, use that ruler on my *bottom*?" I blushed saying this out loud. But he had said it first! I kept going since he just looked at me, his arms folded over that nice broad chest of his. "Is that over the skirt? Is this legal? And my knuckles? Wouldn't that mark me? My husband might wonder."

"Your husband is not my concern, Olivia. How you handle yourself at home is entirely your affair. While you are here at the office, you belong to me. If you are concerned that some possible bruising or mark might be questioned, I would suggest you avail yourself of the second method, that is, your bottom. And yes, first infraction will be over the skirt. After that, we shall see.

"As to legalities, you and I have not entered into any sort of legal contract. I consider what happens here between us to be on both a professional and personal level. That is, I expect you to behave professionally at all times, but our arrangement, by its nature, is personal. Legality doesn't enter into it."

He stood there for a moment, waiting. Maybe he was waiting for me to tell him to go to hell. Waiting to see if I would run out of there screaming. I didn't do either one. I just stood there staring at him like a tongue-tied idiot. Inside I was almost sick with the adrenaline rush I was feeling. My gut was churning like I was on a roller coaster and I felt giddy with anticipation though not really sure of what. I suppose he took my silence for acquiescence, and I guess it was. He went on, with a slight nod of his head, as if I had spoken, as if I had given him permission.

"Now, you have spilled coffee on my desk. That is infraction number one. Then you protested and argued that it was 'just a drop coffee', which clearly indicates to me that you don't value my property in a way that befits your station. That is infraction number two. I shall teach you the value of my things.

"At the end of each day we shall tally your infractions, and I will decide upon a punishment. You will accept the punishment with grace. Failure to comply immediately to my dictate will incur another infraction. Am I clear, Olivia?"

My mouth felt dry. Part of me was furious with this arrogant man. How *dare* he talk to me like I was some kind of servant or slave from medieval times, and he the lord and master of the realm! But most of me was thunderstruck. Yes, that's the word. It's like he was speaking some secret language to me. Some language I didn't know I understood. Something that bypassed my brain and went right to my nerve endings!

I responded in that secret language, I guess. Some kind of weird sense of peace seemed to fall over me as I bowed my head and answered, "Yes, Sir. You are clear, Sir. I apologize about the coffee. I'll be more careful."

"Good," he nodded, looking pleased. "Now get your pad and take a letter. Punishment will be at 4:00 p.m. Sharp."

~*~

A secret language. Tess sat still, staring at the neat writing, the ink pale and fine as insect legs on the page. She found that her mouth was dry, and she swallowed and licked her lips. She had started reading these journals with a sort of superior skepticism. Her sweet, innocent Nana— young Livvie from another era—subjected to the strange perversions of an overstepping boss. At the very least, it was just another hackneyed affair between a man and his secretary.

Yet, Tess found herself getting caught up in the drama of what she was reading. This talk of secret languages and punishments. Tess felt a sweet heat emanating from her pussy at the feelings that were being stirred by the words on the page. She squirmed in her chair, pressing her legs together as she read on.

~*~

October 23, 1961
I've been tempted to take this journal home. Sometimes I write entries in my head, while I'm washing the dishes or doing laundry or whatever. Or later, when Frank and I are lying in bed, the kids finally asleep. I'll be reading my novel as usual, with Frank beside me watching TV and I'll get this ridiculous urge to confide in him. To tell him about the crazy things that are happening at work, and get his opinion!

Can you imagine! Frank would divorce me on the spot, or have me locked in the loony bin. Then he'd go threaten Mr. Stevenson with his stupid shotgun. I bet Mr. Stevenson never shot a deer. No, Mr. Stevenson is not the hunting type—at least not of animals.

I bite my tongue though. I don't say a word, of course. Nothing about my jumble of confused feelings. Nothing about the peculiar arousal I feel when that ruler taps against my chair and I sense Mr. Stevenson's strong, quiet presence behind me.

Mr. Stevenson's right. It would be stupid to leave this journal lying around at home. Beyond stupid. Dangerous. Sometimes I wonder if Mr. Stevenson knows what I'm writing in here. If he knows that I think he looks like Gregory Peck, and that I get all excited and squirmy when he smacks my bottom!

But he doesn't read it. At least he hasn't yet. Maybe I really do have the only key to my desk drawers. I know he hasn't read it so far because I've been doing like they do in those detective novels. I put a strand of my hair very carefully across the cover of the journal. You couldn't really see it unless you were looking for it. And it hasn't been moved. That makes me feel safer, I suppose. These words are just for me.

Well, Friday afternoon was amazing. I didn't incur any additional infractions that day, except one. I think if the truth be told that Mr. Stevenson manufactured that particular infraction in order to increase my punishment. It was during dictation and I swear he said "confidant" but he said no, it was supposed to be "confidence". After lecturing me about being precise in legal documents he said, "Infraction number three."

It was very hard to concentrate for the rest of the afternoon. I didn't do much of anything at all from three-thirty to four o'clock, except check my face in my compact, reapply my lipstick and powder, adjust my stockings, go to the bathroom, fluff my hair. It was like I was going for an audition or on a blind date!

When four o'clock arrived, I wasn't sure if I was just supposed to go in there and bend over or if he was going to come get me. I sat there for about a minute when I heard him call from his office, "Olivia." That's it. Just...Olivia. The door was ajar so I walked in, feeling like I was heading into the principal's office after being caught with cigarettes.

He was sitting at his desk, his pen poised over some document, acting busy. The rat kept looking at his papers, like they were too important to stop reading, even though he was the one who had called me in. I told myself he was just doing that to make me feel more ill at ease—more nervous. More compliant.

Well, it worked! I stood there, trying not to shift and shuffle like a little kid.

Finally, he looked up, as if only suddenly aware that I had entered the room. He looked me slowly up and down. I blushed. I know I did, because I could feel the heat in my face and neck. I tried to stand still—to act calm and collected, like Audrey Hepburn in *Roman Holiday*. And Mr. Stevenson was every bit as handsome as Gregory Peck in that movie. So dashing!

I actually had a sudden fantasy of rushing over and kissing him, right on the mouth! Of course, I didn't! He'd probably have fired me on the spot. I do not believe my crush on Mr. Stevenson is returned. At least not in a schoolboy kind of a way, all gushy and nervous like me. No, he is far too calm and collected for that sort of behavior.

Mr. Stevenson is into control.

He stood up and walked over to the leather couch on the far wall from his desk. He sat down and took his ruler, that ever-present ruler, from the arm of the couch where he'd obviously placed it before, in anticipation of my "punishment".

"Come here, Olivia. How many infractions today?" Like he didn't know.

"Three, Sir," I answered, knowing he would count the confidence/confidant dispute.

"That's correct. For your convenience, I will reiterate the rules of punishment. First infraction—ten strikes—over the skirt or on the knuckles. Second infraction, it becomes twenty. Third infraction, you get to choose.

Thirty strokes of the ruler over your skirt. Or you can choose to only get ten but because of the reduced number, those ten will be under the skirt. Over the panties, but under the skirt."

Well! I pressed my lips together, pretending to weigh my options, but I'd already decided. If we were going to play this game, I thought, then let's do it right! I'll admit something here. I wanted to feel his hand on my bottom. Not my bare bottom! I'm not ready for that. Yet. But the idea of those long, tapered fingers touching my body in such an intimate way, such a dangerous and forbidden way, was somehow deeply exciting to me.

Trying to sound calm I responded, "Ten, under the skirt."

He actually raised his eyebrows, as if he were surprised by my choice. "Very well. Take off the skirt. It's too narrow to hike up."

And I did it! Mrs. Old Married Woman unzipped her skirt and laid it carefully over a chair. I stood there in my girdle and underpants, feeling very self-conscious indeed! Though I feel kind of sorry for his wife—look what he's doing behind her back—in a way knowing that he's married makes me more comfortable. He's obviously seen a woman in this state of undress many times before. Probably doesn't even think twice about it. He looked me over while the heat crept up my cheeks as usual and he said, "I don't like girdles. Why do slender women like you wear girdles?"

Well, I liked that he called me slender! But married or not, he obviously didn't know much about women's undergarments. "To hold up my stockings, of course," I snapped, and then bit my lip, worried I had sounded "impertinent".

He let it pass, answering, "There are much nicer ways to do that, Olivia. Next Monday on your lunch hour, you will go to Slone's Dress Shop in the village and you will pick up a package that I will have them prepare for you. It will be in my name at the counter. You will not wear a girdle again in my presence, once you have the garters that will be waiting for you. Understood?"

The man was buying me underwear! Instead of slapping him in the face and quitting again, I nodded. Garters! I was going to dress like a common whore for this man who was my boss. I knew I was going to do it and I'll admit here, the notion excited me! I would wear these sexy, harlot garter belts at work!

He drew me back to the matter at hand. "Come here and bend over my lap." I did, feeling awkward and sort of ridiculous, a grown woman balancing over a man's knee in her girdle and stockings! But I did it.

Thwack! He smacked me really hard. Much harder than the little taps I'd been getting up until then. "Ouch!" I yelled involuntarily.

"Come now. This is nothing. Take it like a true submissive, Olivia. Silently." Again he smacked me, and I managed not to yelp out loud though I did kind of grunt. I mean, it stung, even through the rubbery fabric of the girdle and my panties. Imagine it on bare skin! Eight more times, covering my entire bottom.

Here's the really weird thing.

The secret thing.

Afterward, my panties were soaked!

I mean, I was so aroused by that paddling that I couldn't wait to get home to Frank! Lucky for me it was Friday, so I was pretty much assured of some sex.

When Frank made love to me, after I finally got the kids off to bed, I think I actually had an orgasm! I'm not exactly sure, but I think I did. Anyway, it felt really good and when he pressed my sore bottom against the sheets, it just made me so hot! I'm sure Frank must have wondered what had gotten into me. He isn't crazy about a woman showing too much emotion during sex. "Isn't seemly", he'd say if pressed. Not that he'd talk about it, but after eleven years, I know that's what he thinks.

I wonder what it's like for Mr. Stevenson and his wife. Does she get punished too? Or would she divorce him if he tried this stuff with her? And where is this going with Mr. Stevenson? Are we having an affair?

What am I doing????

_*_

October 25, 1961

The garters are beautiful. Elegant satin, one in cream, one in black and one in pearl gray. They're so pretty. They must have cost a fortune. The hoity-toity saleslady just looked down her nose at me, but she had the package waiting, all wrapped with pretty ribbon in a lovely box.

I wonder what she thought! Probably figured the little secretary was just picking up a package for the boss. A gift for his wife, perhaps. Well, just imagine if she knew! Anyway, when I got them back to the office, Mr. Stevenson told me to open the package and select a belt. He said I was to leave them at the office each evening, and put one on each morning when I arrived. He said I could wash them out here when necessary.

I wonder if he's done this before. I wonder if Miss Willis was also his "submissive". Maybe someday I'll ask him.

I'm wearing the garters now. The pearl gray ones. It really does feel better than a girdle, though it doesn't "control" my figure as well! I feel almost naked under there. I've been wearing a girdle for so long. I mean, everyone does! Still, I have to admit, it feels really sexy. Right now, as I'm writing, I'm fingering one of the satin ties that attaches to the top of my stocking. It looks really pretty against my bare leg.

I wonder if Mr. Stevenson will ask to see them? I hope so!

_*_

Later—It's four-fifteen and I have to leave in fifteen minutes if I'm to make the bus home in time to cook dinner for Frank and the kids. But I have to write in here for a minute, because I am so annoyed! And confused!

This whole day went by without a hitch. That is, no infractions. We were just like two regular people working in an office. "Good morning, Olivia." "Good morning, Mr. Stevenson." I was very careful, typed everything perfectly, took excellent dictation, set the coffee down with precision and care, and was a model employee.

I kept half-expecting him to call me in and ask to see the garters. I mean, he paid for them! He called me in late in the morning to dictate a few letters. I was sure this was it, and he would ask me to lift my skirt and show him the garters, just to prove I'd followed his instructions. Not a word. He dictated several letters and then simply said, "Thank you, Olivia, that will be all." I even stood there for a few seconds, waiting for him to look up again and start to speak.

Well, he did look up, but all he said was, "Was there something else, Olivia?" I had to bite my tongue, let me tell you. Mr. Stevenson has yet to experience my sarcastic side. I lost my nerve though, muttering, "No, Sir. I'll get back to my desk and get these typed up."

When 4:00 came, I thought, well, this is it! Now he'll call me in to show him the sexy garters. I even admonished myself that I should have realized it'd be at 4:00—"punishment time". Of course, that makes sense, since earlier in the day might be too distracting for both of us, and we do have a law office to run!

Well, 4:00 came and went and nothing happened. Just now Mr. Stevenson came out of his office, barely stopping, and said, "Good night, Olivia." That's it! Just good night! He took his overcoat and his hat, and, after reminding me to lock up, left!

Now I'm sitting here, just fuming! How insane is that? I was waiting for the game, and he didn't play! Maybe it isn't a game at all for Mr. Stevenson. Maybe he really just wants me to behave "properly" and when I do, that's the end of it. He didn't even check to see if I was wearing my garters. Is the man made of flesh and blood or stone and metal? Aren't I an attractive woman?

Here I am, all furious, because my boss didn't smack me with a ruler. Angry because I was waiting around all day like an idiot for him to call me in and demand to see the garters he paid for. There is definitely something wrong with me. I wonder if I should see a doctor. I better get home.

chapter 3

October 26, 1961

WEDNESDAY MORNING I got here early, before Mr. Stevenson, so I could put on my garters. I wore the black ones, with the pair of sheer black stockings I usually only wear when Frank and I go out somewhere fancy. Whether or not he was going to look at them, I'd decided I was going to wear them! I also decided that if I had anything to do with it, I was going to get that man to look at them.

When Mr. Stevenson came in that morning, after the usual pleasantries he said, "I need the Masterson file right away. And a cup of coffee, if you please." Now, normally, I would have jumped up and gotten that file and brought it to him right away. Then off to the kitchenette to pour him a cup and make it just the way he likes it, one sugar and plenty of cream. But not too much cream, or the coffee won't be hot enough.

Well, I didn't do either thing! I pretended to make a phone call, actually calling First Fidelity for that recording of time and temperature. Then I buffed a nail and reapplied my lipstick. Then, and only then, I got the file he wanted, but oops, it was the Masters file, instead of the Masterson!

I chickened out when it actually came to spilling coffee on purpose—God knows I don't want to be the one responsible for destroying his family heirloom—but there was probably too much cream in the coffee. I left the cup and saucer on his desk. He didn't look up or act as if he knew I existed. I went back to my desk.

After a while, Mr. Stevenson came out and got the proper file himself, dumping the wrong one in front of me. But still he hadn't said a word.

The morning went on as any other and at lunchtime, I half expected him to say something, but still not a word. I was too nervous to eat my lunch! Here I'd gone and messed things up on purpose, just to see what he would do, and he didn't do a thing! The afternoon took about fifteen hours to go by, but at 4:00 on the nose I heard, "Olivia."

I got up and went in, having already adjusted my stockings and checked my makeup. I was going to get my little spanking now! But Mr. Stevenson isn't so easy to manipulate! That's what I found out today.

I'm not even exactly sure what happened, but I figure if I write it down here, it will help me sort it out. When I entered the office, Mr. Stevenson said, "Close the door." He's never said that before, since we are the only two in the office, but I obeyed, wondering what was going to be different, but of course not daring to ask.

He just stood there behind his chair for a while, looking me up and down. "The mouse," he finally said with just the ghost of a smile, "is toying with the cat. The mouse," he went on, "likes to play, and sees this all as a little game.

The mouse—" now he stared at me until I blushed and looked down, "—will have to learn this is no game."

Well, I was squirming like a kid again and wishing I could start the day over. What had I been thinking! Sophisticated Mr. Stevenson wasn't going to fall for my obvious little ploys! Now he said, "Olivia, you do need to be punished. That much is clear. Not because you brought me the wrong file, but because you did it on purpose. Not because my coffee tasted too bland, but because you did that on purpose as well.

"You are toying with me. Some clarifications apparently need to be made. You will need to be taught that it is I, not you, who initiates punishments, who decides what is and what is not an infraction, and who decides how you will behave when you are here. Go to the corner."

"What?"

"Go to the corner, and put your nose against the wall. Women who act like naughty little girls will be treated as such. You willfully tried to manipulate me into using a ruler on you, like a kid trying to trick her daddy into buying her candy. So, go on, little girl. Nose against the wall. Hands behind your back. Grab each elbow with the opposite hand and stand perfectly still. Go on. Do it, or get out."

Well, I wasn't going to obey such a ridiculous order. You can bet I wasn't going to! But something in his tone compelled me to obey! My legs felt like rubber, but somehow I got myself over to the corner. In an almost trance-like state, I leaned over, touching my nose to the wall. He made me stand out further from the wall, so that I had to stick out my rear to keep my nose in place. I was mortified! That's the best word for it. Mortified and humiliated.

And on fire.

I felt so ridiculous there, with my nose pressed against the wall, holding my hands behind my back. But that tingle was there too! I realized I was waiting for him to come up behind me. To press slowly against me, like in the movies, and maybe let my bun down or something. I don't know what exactly I was expecting.

Stop lying, Livvie. You know exactly what you were expecting, or even hoping would happen.

I fantasized right there on the spot that he would lean over me and kiss my neck, and maybe whisper something sexy about me belonging to him. My ears were pricked, waiting to hear him approach. I was so excited, even though I felt so silly with my face in the corner. Something was about to happen! He could say what he liked about manipulation, but here I was, waiting for the exciting, sexy, dangerous thing to happen!

Well, it didn't. Nothing. Zippo. Just me standing there, my nose against the wall, feeling more and more ridiculous. I got a crick in my neck and my legs were tired, still in my pumps. My arms started to ache as I tried to balance with my nose while holding my elbows behind me! He just stood there, or whatever he was doing. For all I knew, he had left!

I stayed in the corner for three hours. No, it couldn't have been, but it felt like it! At 4:28 he said, "Good night, Olivia. I'll see you in the morning. Try a stunt like that again and see where it takes you." The bastard walked out of his office and left for the night!

I had to scramble and I barely made the bus, running and shouting for it to wait. If thoughts could kill, the man would not have made it home in his fancy Lincoln. He would have died of "natural causes" before his wife could serve him his meatloaf!

~*~

Tess found herself grinning, even through her shock. Now, that sounded like the Nana she knew. But the rest of it? It was a lot to take in. Her grandmother had been living a secret life, a life none of them knew about, for who knew how long?

Tess knew she was going to read all of Nana's secret diaries. And then what was she going to do? Tell her mom or her sisters? No. Never. Nana and Tess shared many secrets, most of them just little things, but all of them dear to Tess's heart.

Nana had never told anyone about the time Tess had shoplifted in fourth grade and gotten caught. The man at the store had taken pity on little Tess who stood sobbing, clutching the book of paper dolls she had stared at for twenty minutes before suddenly swiping and trying to secure beneath her windbreaker. Terror at what she had done drove her from the store at a run. She couldn't have been more obvious if she'd screamed aloud as she ran, "I stole this! I stole this!"

The shopkeeper had run out after her, calling, "Little girl! Little girl!" And, mortified, she had stopped, clutching the book under her jacket, tears already streaming down her face. He had taken pity on her, only making her hand it back and promise not to do that again. It couldn't have been a stronger lesson, and Tess had been cured on the spot of shoplifting.

But in her child's mind, a sense of guilt overwhelmed her, as well as a need to confess to someone. Her mother? Even at that young age, Tess sensed that her mother would not have been as forgiving as the man in the store had been. Tess envisioned a spanking at the very least, and quite possibly, a huge story blown up all out of proportion by the time her father came home, late as usual and smelling of whiskey.

Then off would come his belt and little Tess would pay a heavy price for her bad deed. So she had stayed silent, huddled in her bed in the room she shared with her sister, Stacy. She had confided in no one for three days.

But when Saturday finally came and she went to spend the morning with Nana, helping her in her garden and baking cookies, the words had come tumbling out at last, like a wound that had needed lancing to heal.

Tess knew instinctively that Nana wouldn't betray her and tell her parents. No, Nana had scooped her up in her arms and let her cry out her shame, and then asked her, "And will you do such a silly thing again, Nicky sweetheart?"

And as Tess shook her head fervently, Nana kissed her round, wet little cheek and said, "No, I know you won't, and no harm was done, so let's put it behind us, dear. Now, would you like some of these delicious cookies? I think they're just about done!"

Tess sat now smiling, remembering the person in her life who had been most loving and most understanding. How could she reconcile that woman with the sexy secretary in the journal, who seemed to be describing the beginnings of a very bizarre love affair?

And Mr. Stevenson. James Stevenson, who was still alive, and had maintained contact with Nana—with Olivia. Tess toyed with the idea of calling him back. But what would she say?

"I found those diaries, and know all about your kinky affair with my grandmother. Explain yourself." What right had she to demand any explanations? Nana had been an adult, making her own decisions before Tess was even a glimmer in her own mother's eye.

It was so much to take in.

Maybe Brad would have some insight.

Should she even tell Brad?

Tess smiled dreamily, her mind drifting to her new boyfriend. Could she call him that? They'd only been dating a few weeks now, since the week after Nana had passed away in fact. But she felt closer to him than to any man she'd been with before, even her last serious lover, Jordan. That had lasted two years, and for a while, she had been convinced he was "the one". That is, until she found him in bed with Janet Parker, his upstairs neighbor.

Brad Hunter, age twenty-eight, was an attorney just like Tess. They were both known as go-getters in the law firm of Reilly & Clark, though Brad was further along in his career. Tess had only been with the firm for a close to a year, recruited straight out of law school.

It was only these past few months that she and Brad had started getting to know one another. Long days and nights thrown together when they were both given the Joseph Tool Company lawsuit to prepare had given them time, professionally and otherwise, to check each other out.

When the case was over, Tess found she had more than just friendly feelings toward Brad. He was good-looking and hard-working, a promising combination in her book. From what she could gather from their occasional personal conversations between legal briefs and research, he wasn't married and didn't have a steady girlfriend. She had wanted to get to know him better, but he tended to be so focused at work that they hadn't really had much time for small talk.

She had invited him out for dinner one Friday, making it seem as if it was a last-minute idea of hers, though she'd been mulling the idea over in her mind for a few days. If nothing else, she wanted to distract herself from her sad thoughts of her grandmother, whose sweet smile she would never see again.

That Friday morning, just in case, she had worn a sexy new thong and matching bra, not that she expected him to see it, but just in case. And just in case, she made sure the apartment was clean and neat, with fresh sheets on the bed. Not that she expected him to come back to her place, much less get into her bed, but just in case.

When six o'clock rolled around, Brad was still bent over his desk, his sleeves rolled up midway against the sexy muscles of his forearms. His dark brown hair flopped over his forehead, and he had a pen dangling from his mouth. His desk was covered in papers.

Unlike Tess, who worked meticulously and neatly on one thing at a time, Brad was known for spreading out over every available surface, balancing twenty things in his head at a time and somehow pulling it all together. She didn't understand his work habits, but she had to admit he produced the goods. He was definitely on the fast track for a junior partnership.

Peeking around his door, and trying to tell herself it was cool whichever way it went, Tess said in a casual tone, "Hey, Brad. It's Friday. I was thinking of popping over to that new Indian place to check it out. Any chance you'd like to join me?"

She'd said it! They weren't working on any projects together, so this wasn't just a quick bite between assignments. She was asking him out. The ball was in his court. Either he'd look up and say, "Sure, why not", or he'd sigh and say, "Gee, I'd love to, but I'm swamped here. Maybe in a year or two..."

"Sure, that's a great idea. I've been staring at the same legal opinion for the past twenty minutes! My brain is totally fried. I could definitely go for some Saag Paneer and Rogan Josh about now!"

So they'd gone for Indian and lots of red wine, and when the meal was over, Brad had turned to Tess and said, "I'd invite you over, but my roommate's girlfriend seems to have kind of moved in lately, and I've no idea what we might stumble in on!"

This left Tess the obvious opening, "Well, we could go to my place. No roommates. Just Butterscotch."

"Butterscotch?"

"My cat." Somehow this was funny—maybe it was all that wine, and they laughed until the tears rolled. Then Tess paid the bill, insisting, as she had been the one to extend the invitation. Brad grinned, ducking his head gracefully and said the next one was on him. He followed her in his car to her neighborhood, which was only a few miles from the restaurant.

Sitting back on her overstuffed couch, Tess was stunned to discover it was one o'clock in the morning. They'd talked for hours, sharing stories about their work, their childhoods, their families, their lives, and Tess felt as if they'd been friends forever.

When talk had turned to Nana, and her death only the week before, Brad had held Tess in his arms, smoothing away her tears and kissing her lightly on her forehead. She had half expected him to make a move at that point, using the tenderness of the moment to move down to her lips, to move from the chaste brotherly kiss to a lover's kiss.

When he didn't, she was at once relieved and annoyed. She liked that he was a gentleman and hadn't taken advantage, but found that a part of her had been poised and ready for that kiss, even behind tears that were real.

Instead, he'd patted her and held her some more. The conversation slowly eased into lighter things and they gossiped for a few minutes about the people they worked with. The talk ebbed into an easy silence.

Finally, Brad said, "Tess. You know, this has been the most fun I've had in years. I can't believe we didn't connect before this. I get so bogged down in my work, so obsessed about making partner that I forget what's really important. Thanks for taking the first step and asking me out. I hope it's the first step of many between us."

He stood, stretching and then leaned down, taking her easily into his arms. He kissed her, his lips sweet and warm against hers, but only for a moment or two. She wrapped her arms around him, pulling him into her, pressing her tongue against his lips so that they parted. She had expected him to seize the moment and accept her unspoken invitation to stay.

But again, it was he who pulled away. Instead of asking where the bedroom was, he said, "Can I call you tomorrow? I was going to go in to the office but I think I'd much rather spend the day with you, unless, of course, you have plans." He smiled at her, a wide smile that revealed a dimple in his left cheek. She couldn't help but grin back, even though part of her felt deflated by his obvious ending of the evening.

"Sure. I was going to go over to my grandmother's this weekend and start to clean it out. My mom asked me if I would. But it can wait another week. I don't really have the heart for it, to tell you the truth."

They spent a wonderful day, starting with pancakes and sausage at the waffle house, moving on to stroll in the botanical gardens and then taking in a matinee movie and sharing a late lunch. Tess felt like they'd been together forever and yet they'd barely even kissed. In the movie theater, he'd put his arm loosely around her shoulders, and Tess had leaned into him, loving the smell of him, the scent of his cologne and his own essence.

That afternoon he'd left her frustrated again, apologizing that he had promised his mom he'd take her to dinner that night, as his dad was out of town on business. Again, he'd asked if he could call and this time the kiss was long and lingering, leaving her literally weak in the knees.

That night alone in bed, she touched herself, imagining those were Brad's fingers caressing her sex, touching her breasts. It was lonely business, but it did the job, at least enough for her to fall asleep.

The next week during work, they barely saw one another, each one piled high with caseloads and paperwork. But they spoke each night on the telephone and had made a date for that Saturday night. Brad was going to take her out this time, to his favorite Japanese place. Tess, never having tried sushi, was a little leery, but willing.

They sat together on the same side of a low black lacquer table, sitting directly on the tatami mat in their stocking feet. They were in a private little room with rice paper windows and a sliding rice paper door. A little brightly colored paper lantern hung from the ceiling, throwing off a muted, romantic light.

A lithe young Japanese woman, dressed in traditional kimono garb and padded little socks with a split between the big and second toe, glided into the room, bringing a pot of hot green tea and a bottle of hot sake. Tess let Brad do the ordering and after the waitress had poured the drinks, they were left alone in the little room.

Tess picked up the little ceramic cup and sipped. "It's good!" she exclaimed. "I never thought I'd like hot wine, but then I never thought I'd eat raw fish either."

Brad laughed, and told her sushi and sashimi were his favorite foods, even better than Indian. He was delighted when the pretty plate of artfully prepared food was brought in and he smiled at the young woman, saying something in Japanese.

Tess was impressed as the Japanese woman blushed and bowed, responding in kind. Brad laughed it off and said, "Oh, I just said 'thank you'. That and 'good morning' are about all I know." Taking up a pair of chopsticks with practiced ease, Brad said, "Now, here's how you eat it. You take a little of this, this is pickled ginger, and a little of this green stuff. It's called wasabi. It's a kind of horseradish, and you have to be careful not to use too much or you'll get what I call a wasabi rush. Let's try some tuna first. That's my favorite."

Brad loaded a little bit of red, raw tuna and rice with the condiments and handed it to Tess, who took it with some trepidation. Smiling bravely, she took a bite. She chewed a moment and pronounced, "This is delicious!"

Brad grinned, and together they ate platefuls of fish and drank several small bottles of sake. "Whew!" Tess said, leaning heavily against him. "That stuff is strong! I don't even know if I can stand up!"

Somehow, they managed to make their way to the car and Brad drove Tess to her place. "Aren't you coming in?" she asked, her voice almost a whine.

"Oh, Tess, I'm sorry. I think I got you drunk! I forgot how sake goes to some people's heads. I'm a little tipsy myself. I'm afraid if I come in, I don't know where we might end up!"

"Brad," maybe the alcohol had loosened her tongue, but Tess spoke just exactly what was on her mind. "I get the distinct feeling you are avoiding having sex with me. If that's the case, just come out and say it! I'm a big girl, I can take it. But all this coy shit is driving me up the wall! Are we dating or not? What is it, are you gay? Oh, God, don't tell me you're gay!"

Brad stared at her, and then burst out laughing. She laughed too, though she wasn't sure what they were laughing at. If only the wine hadn't muddled her head so! "No, I'm not gay, you little idiot! I can't believe you'd even ask me that. I am taking my time with you! Because I care about you, Tess. Because I have a history of jumping into bed with girls, thinking I'm head over heels, and in a couple of weeks I have no idea what the hell I'm doing with them, and they usually feel the same way.

"We've got something, you and me. I don't know what it is yet, but it's definitely something, and I don't want to ruin it by fucking you first, and getting to know you later."

Tess stared at him a moment, his face silhouetted against the streetlights. She stared at his strong hands, the fingers gripped still on the steering wheel. He was looking at her, his expression obscured in the shadows.

"Fuck that," she said, laughing. "I want you now! I don't want to wait anymore. In fact, I can't wait another second! We know each other. I'm begging you, baby. Fuck me! Take me upstairs and fuck my brains out. If you don't, I'm going to have to rape you right here!"

Brad stared at Tess a moment, and she knew, even through the fog of rice wine, that she'd probably gone too far. Slowly a smile curved its way over his face and he lunged toward her, kissing her passionately until she literally lost her breath. Jumping from the car, he raced around to her side and almost pulled her from the seat.

Tess didn't remember how they got into the apartment, or how they got to the bed. She did remember his consideration, when he asked her if she had protection and she told him she was on the pill. And most especially she remembered him, naked and beautiful, rearing up in front of her like a satyr, broad and strong, before he plunged into her, ravaging her, taking her, claiming her.

He made love to her like someone desperate for the lifeblood that their sex seemed to offer a dying man. He pumped into her, holding her wrists high above her head. She was completely captive beneath him, at the mercy of his rock-hard cock thrusting and slamming into her.

He came, calling her name, his body so hot on top of hers she thought he might combust. Then slowly, once his pounding heart had returned closer to normal, he slid down off her, letting her wrists go, kissing her breasts, tonguing the nipples, circling them in teasing swirls and edging down her belly, to her sex.

She lay still, plundered and open to him. Gently he tasted her, the taste of the two of them, and moved up to her little clit, erect and eager for his kiss. He pressed her thighs farther apart with his strong hands and when she instinctively tried to close them, he wouldn't let her. He was much stronger than she and besides she didn't really want to close her legs, as his tongue was like warm, silky perfection against her heated needy body.

He teased her mercilessly, always holding her legs wide, sometimes licking and suckling, sometimes gently biting, sometimes just blowing his sweet breath against her. He seemed to know just how far to take her so that she teetered over a sharp, sensual edge, before he would pull her back, denying her the release she felt she desperately needed.

For Tess, she had to admit, the turn-on was as much what he withheld as what he gave. Brad played her like an instrument, knowing just when to drum her gently, just when to strum and play her until she was burning with passion, her entire being focused entirely on Brad, and what he was doing to her.

Finally, he took pity on the panting, moaning girl, now begging in a litany of lust for him to make her come. Arching up, Tess pulled his head against her, gripping handfuls of his hair, crying and laughing at the same time, tears spilling down her cheeks, her heart splitting open with something that felt very much like love.

chapter 4

THEY WERE SNUGGLED in bed together, taking turns reading aloud. Tess had found herself torn at first, as she debated internally over whether to share her grandmother's secret. Things felt different though, now that Brad had made love to her. She found herself thinking over and over of how he had claimed her. It had been a surprise, but deeply exciting, when he'd held her arms, his strong hands tight around each wrist, pinning her to the bed, impaling her with his hard cock.

She had experienced a deep sensual thrill at his physical dominance. It was almost as if they had spoken a secret language with their bodies.

A secret language.

Just as Olivia had felt with Mr. Stevenson. It was that connection in her mind that made Tess decide to share her bizarre discovery with Brad. She'd let him read up to where she had left off, after explaining how she'd discovered the journals in the first place and giving him a thumbnail sketch of the Nana she knew compared to the woman who had written the words unfolding on the pages before them.

Brad had listened, amazement registering on his face as Tess described what she had found. He smiled, his eyes twinkling. "So Livvie had a secret life? Sounds exotic. Imagine." He drew a finger along Tess's cheek, "Living one life at home, the typical working mother with the typical boring marriage, while at work a secret world of sexual submission and increasingly bizarre demands is opening up for her. I guess it must be strange for you, knowing it was your grandmother that penned those words, so long ago."

"He's still alive, you know. He called the house."

"Who?"

And so, Tess explained about the mysterious phone call, and the sound of his breaking voice as he hung up, not even asking for any specifics. "I've been wondering if I should call him back," she mused aloud. "He hung up before I could tell him much. He didn't even ask about the funeral."

"His wife may still be alive, don't forget," Brad said. "We don't know anything about his circumstances now, or if it would be seemly for such a man to attend the funeral of a secretary who used to work for him once upon a time."

Tess thought about it, nodding slowly. "I guess you're right. Still, I would love to talk to him sometime, if I could get up the nerve. I think I'll just save that phone number from the caller ID. Just in case."

"Good plan, counselor. Keep the evidence for future discovery by the court. Let's read on, shall we?"

_*_

October 31, 1961

Well, he finally asked to see the garters I've been wearing for a week now. I had no warning. I had decided by then that he wasn't going to ask, and that was that. I even considered putting my girdle back on, since it does give me a tidier figure. But truth to tell, there's something very sexy about sliding those stockings slowly up my legs in the bathroom at work. Knowing he might one day knock while I was in the middle of it! I imagine us in some kind of sultry film noir, my leg raised provocatively as I ease the soft silk up a firm calf, and he watches, mesmerized.

Of course, I actually put them on before he even gets to the office, so fat chance of that happening! Nevertheless, I guess it's a good thing that I continued with the little ritual. Mr. Stevenson says rituals are important, and will become more a part of my training as time goes on. He drives me crazy when he says things like that, and then refuses to elaborate. "Patience is a virtue," he says, smiling that sardonic smile of his.

This morning he called me in with his usual one-word command.

"Olivia."

"Coming, Sir," I said, just finishing a sentence on my typewriter.

He was sitting at his desk as usual, as I came to stand in front of it, trying to appear calm, though I recognized from the tone of his "Olivia" that his request wasn't going to have to do with the law practice. I was right.

"Take off your skirt."

I hadn't been expecting that! Lamely I said, "Excuse me?"

"Do I need to repeat myself? Am I unclear?"

"Well, um, it's just you haven't asked that before, I mean, not since that punishment, and I don't think I've got any infractions today—"

"You do now. Don't question me. Do as you're told."

Well, I did. Part of me was chastising myself in my head. See, I told myself, you wanted this! You wanted him to look at your garters, and now he's doing it, so what's your problem? I think I hesitated because it was sudden, so unexpected, and I felt rather shy. But he sat there, looking so stern, and as if what he was asking was nothing out of the ordinary.

This is it, I thought. No turning back now. He's going to make love to me, oh, my God. Slowly, I slipped out of my skirt, hoping against hope I wouldn't trip in my heels and make a fool of myself. I noticed my hand was trembling when I lay the skirt and slip over the back of a chair. I stood there in my garters and stockings, and of course my panties, bra and blouse, feeling nervous as a colt. I made myself stand still, realizing I was fidgeting and moving from foot to foot.

Instead of looking pleased, or at least lecherous, the man looked horrified. I know I blushed, my ears even got hot! How dare he look at me that way! I mean, I know I'm not nineteen anymore, but I'm not a cow! I felt my indignation rising when he said, "What is that ridiculous underwear?"

Can you imagine! First of all, they aren't ridiculous! They're just nice practical cotton underpants. Does he think I have drawers full of satin little bikini panties like those young models are wearing? I'm a grown woman! I've had three children! I retorted something along those lines and I swear I could almost see a little smile attempting to escape.

He continued. "Olivia, I don't want to see those faded cotton briefs in here ever again, do you understand? It goes the way of the girdle. I will have another package prepared for you at Slone's tomorrow." He pursed his lips, looking thoroughly disgusted. I felt humiliated and not a little chagrined. Not a word about my legs, which I know are still nice, or the garters, or the fact that I had obeyed him without protest and taken off the skirt.

I tell you, the man is driving me to distraction. If only I knew where Distraction was located!

Later—the workday almost over. Just time to write a few words here. Mr. Stevenson called me in again and gave me detailed instructions about Slone's. I'm to go over as soon as they open. I'm to ask for Miss Reynolds and tell her I'm there about the package for Mr. Stevenson. He says she will tell me exactly what to do and I must obey her to the letter. He says he will receive a full report from her and that I am to behave as if she were his mouthpiece. Can you imagine! His mouthpiece. What do I see in this man?

~*~

Brad laughed. "Olivia was a piece of work! This stuff is incredible! So hot but so funny, all at the same time. Jesus, I would have loved a secretary like that."

Tess looked at him, not sure how much of what he was saying was a joke. So hot? Was he turned on by the developing D/s relationship between Olivia and Mr. Stevenson?

So far, they hadn't discussed the precise nature of whatever was developing between them along those lines. While Brad was definitely dominant in the bedroom in a way that deeply excited Tess, he had yet to come out and say, "I want to dom you, Tess."

And she had never openly admitted she adored the way he took her, forcefully or gently, but always completely under his control. He set the pace and he decided when she would orgasm, or even if she would orgasm. It was always he that brought her over the edge and she adored the whole dynamic, feeling more alive and vital than ever before. But so far it had been tacit between them. So far, they were silent on the matter.

Brad put his arm around Tess, his fingers reaching for her nipple, squeezing it through the thin fabric of the camisole she was wearing. Tess shivered with pleasure and pressed closer to him. As they continued to read, Brad shifted, his cock rising hard against her.

~*~

November 1, 1961
This may have been the strangest day so far. I left at 10:00 in the morning, right in the middle of our workday, as Mr. Stevenson had instructed. I went right over to the counter and asked for a Miss Reynolds.

After a nervous moment, as that same old biddy looked down her long nose at me, a plump but sweet-looking young woman came out from the back and held out her hand to me. She said, "Oh, you must be Olivia. I am Miss Reynolds. Mr. Stevenson said to expect you. Please come back to our private fitting area. I'm all ready for you." Well, the snooty saleslady seemed impressed and as I glanced back at her, she was actually doing some kind of grimace with her face that I think was meant to be a smile.

As we were walking back to the fitting area, I was struck by the woman's usage of my first name, but then calling herself "Miss Reynolds". Rather uppity of her, I thought, though she had seemed most gracious. It was odd. I didn't particularly know what to do about it, so I decided not to worry about it.

She unlocked a little door that was covered in brocaded pink satin, very posh, and we entered, she gesturing graciously for me to go in first. It was a rather large fitting room and there was an array of soft satin items on a low counter. There was a large chair, which Miss Reynolds sat in as she said, "I've brought a few things in for you to try. Mr. Stevenson did give me some direction, but he trusts my discretion. Now that I see you—" she stood again and walked to the fancy underwear she'd laid out, "—I think we should try this one, and this, and this." She picked up these tiny little bits of satin and handed them to me.

I stood there, confused. Was she suggesting I try on underwear? And while she stood there? "I'm sorry," I ventured. "I don't understand."

"Oh, my apologies," she said smoothly, smiling in a rather superior but still kindly way. "Mr. Stevenson instructed me to treat you as usual." I just stared at her and she colored very slightly, and then went on, "He, uh, didn't tell you what to do?"

I thought back to what he had said. "Mouthpiece" came back to me, and his instruction that I do whatever Miss Reynolds said to do, and "obey her to the letter". I felt funny, suddenly, realizing there must be something between these two, between Mr. Stevenson and Miss Reynolds. Some kind of "understanding" about the girls he sent to be "treated as usual".

Now I was the one to blush and I blurted out, "He said to, um, obey you to the letter. That's what he said." I looked down, feeling very young and very strange. I considered walking out of that fancy fitting room right then.

I felt Miss Reynolds' cool hand on my arm and in her warm voice she said, "Please, Olivia, relax. I can see this is new for you. You aren't sure what to expect. Mr. Stevenson has a way of tossing his girls into things."

Well, I just had to interrupt. "Excuse me. But what are you talking about? His girls? What girls? What is this?" Miss Reynolds looked at me with a funny expression on her face. "Pardon me, Olivia. I need to make a quick phone call. Please wait just a moment. I'll be right back." She slipped out of the room. I didn't know what to think! My glance fell on the pretty lingerie and I went over to look at the pieces she'd selected for me.

They truly were lovely. Heavy satin, beautifully sewn in dark creamy beige, black and crimson. I touched the fabric to my cheek, enjoying the smooth soft slide of it on my skin. There were panties and little matching camisoles. This stuff was expensive! Probably cost more than my whole outfit! But hey, it was Mr. Stevenson's dime.

She came back in after a few minutes and said, "I've talked to Mr. Stevenson. I understand things better now. I wasn't entirely clear. He did explain the, uh, newness, of your situation. Mr. Stevenson says we are to take our time, so don't worry about hurrying back to the office."

Sitting down again she said, "Mr. Stevenson said you are to try on the things I select and model them for me. He trusts my taste."

"Try them on? Panties? In front of you?"

"Oh," she waved her hand airily, like this was an everyday thing, which perhaps for her, it was. "Don't be shy. This is my profession. I have an eye for these things. But if you'd be more comfortable, you can change there." She pointed to a little curtained-off area. "Mr. Stevenson says you are to leave on the garters and stockings. And of course, you can leave on your brassiere, but do remove everything else. Otherwise, we won't get the full effect. Don't worry about leaving on your old underwear. I'm so sure these were made for you, I want to see them as they were meant to be worn." She handed me the flimsy pieces and I took them, stepping behind the curtain.

What was I doing there? In the middle of the work-day, trying on fancy lingerie in Slone's, which I would never have even walked into otherwise! And then I was going to model it for this "Miss Reynolds"—this "mouthpiece" for my boss-come-lover?

Is he becoming my lover? And how many women has he had before me? How many will come after?

He's never touched me, except under the guise of "inspecting" me. We've never shared a kiss, much less anything else! I call him Mr. Stevenson, for heaven's sake! And yet there I was, trying on these pretty panties because he had told me my old underwear had to go.

It sounds ridiculous to me as I sit here writing this, and yet there it is. I can't deny there's something going on between us. Something very strange, but I will admit it, very exciting.

_*_

The little notebook fell aside as Brad's mouth found Tess's. They kissed for several minutes. When he finally let her go, he whispered, "It's about control."

"What?" Tess's hair was wild around her face, her eyes over-bright. Brad put his hand lightly on her chest. Her heart was pounding, her breathing ragged and shallow. It took all his self-control not to rip the satin from her body and plunge into her.

He forced himself to pull away, leaning up on one elbow. Through heavy-lidded eyes, he surveyed Tess—her disheveled hair, her nipples poking hard through her nightshirt, her lips parted and glistening from his kisses. She wanted what he wanted—he was sure of it. Now was the time to put words to it.

"I said it's about control. That's what's turning her on. What's turning you on. It's primordial. You understand it without words. Her secret language. Our secret language too, hmm, Tess?" She shivered and ducked her head, but not before he saw the knowledge in her eyes.

He kissed her again, this time slamming her down against the pillows, lifting her arms far above her head and holding them there. Feeling his power like a drug in his veins, Brad held both slender wrists in one hand, slipping the fingers of his other hand into the panties that covered her swollen, wet pussy.

He groaned with lust as he opened her sex, which was wet and swollen beneath his fingers. She moaned against his lips and tongue, grinding against his fingers.

"Fuck me," she murmured.

"No," he said simply. They kissed a little longer, while he waited for the words to register.

When they did, Tess pulled back with a petulant, confused look. "What?" She clearly wasn't used to a man turning her down for sex.

Brad laughed. He had her just where he wanted her. "You're a little slut, Tess. You want it so bad you'll do anything to get it, won't you?"

Tess drew in her breath, shocked outrage forming on her face. "How dare you! No one talks to me like that! What's your problem?" She struggled against him, trying to wrench her wrists free from his firm grasp. He held her easily, amused and aroused by her struggles.

Failing to break free, she twisted her body away from him. Using his free hand, he turned her face back toward him. She was flushed, though with embarrassment or arousal he couldn't quite say. Both, he suspected. He leaned over her, putting his mouth over hers, forcing her lips apart as she tried to turn her head, to get away from him.

The struggle dissolved as she began to kiss him back, sighing against his lips, arching her body up to his. She wanted this, as much as he did, he was certain. She was longing for precisely the same kind of control Mr. Stevenson had exerted over Olivia so long ago. Only Tess and Brad could be more direct with each other, more honest. They were free to explore their burgeoning D/s passions without worry of censure, or of destroying anyone's marriage.

Brad pulled at the flimsy camisole, lifting it to find Tess's soft, round breast and the hard little nipple at its center. He teased and tugged at it, before leaning down to lick and lightly bite it. Tess's struggle ceased completely, her nipple hardening like a marble in his mouth.

He whispered, "It's lovely that you're a slut, Tess. Please don't take it as an insult. I want you to be my beautiful slut. To give yourself over to me, completely. Remember what I said. It's about control. Your need to be controlled. Olivia needed to be controlled. I can show you what was happening there, darling, if you'll let me. I can see from your reactions as we read, that you understand on some level what your grandmother is beginning to experience in those pages. I can see that you not only understand, but are deeply aroused by it, though you may not have the experience or vocabulary yet to express it."

Tess's eyes opened and she stared at Brad, but said nothing. Interpreting her silence as agreement, Brad continued. "It's amazing you found this record of a Dominant/submissive relationship from forty years ago. And it was someone you knew. Not only knew, but loved and valued.

"If you can get past that, that she was someone's grandma, and that she obviously had an affair, this is an incredible piece of history we're holding here." Brad traced a line along Tess's cheek then dragged his finger farther down. "I think it's wonderful that you felt safe enough with me to share this secret diary. And I think it's only fair that I open up now with you too."

Tess tensed. He could feel her expectancy. Everything in her body language said she was ready to hear what he had to say, and so, in a leap of trust, Brad determined to confide in his new lover.

"You and I, we both connect with what's happening between Olivia and Mr. Stevenson. I find myself holding my breath before each entry, wondering how far they'll dare to go today. Because you know it's a matter of time, don't you, Tess?"

He leaned in again, kissing her, sure she took his double meaning, that it was only a matter of time before they, too, realized their potential D/s relationship. "Take off your panties," he whispered, delighted when she at once obeyed.

Pushing apart her silky-smooth thighs, Brad stroked the swelling petals of her wet cunt. He pressed a finger inside her, enjoying the grip of her muscles massaging it. "I want you, Tess. Not just for a lover. I want more. I demand more."

"Yes," she whispered. And again, "Yes."

Brad's cock was stiff as iron. He touched the tip of it to her wet softness and pressed into the willing girl. She moaned, her cunt closing around him like a snug, hot glove. Nothing had ever felt so good in his life.

He wanted to thrust deep inside her; to pummel her, to use her without regard for her pleasure or her need. But he held back. He needed to know for sure. He needed her to say the words. "Do you want it too, Tess? You don't have to understand it all now. We have time. All the time we need. But do you want me? Are you willing to let go, to give over control to me? To take what I give you?"

Unable to resist, he punctuated the word "take" with a savage thrust into Tess's tight little pussy. She jerked against him with a cry and began to rut like a bitch in heat against him. He very nearly came from her wanton movements, forcing himself under control until she spoke.

"Answer me," he urged.

"Yes!" she screamed, clutching him as if she'd slide away otherwise, her face contorted in orgasm, her cunt milking his cock with its orgasmic spasms until he, too, came with a cry of pleasure, Tess's name on his lips.

chapter 5

November 7, 1961

I'VE BEEN WAITING for this to happen. I knew it was just a matter of time. Now that it has, I'm not sure what to think. I can't fool myself anymore about what is or isn't happening between us. And if this was just a game before, albeit a bizarre one, it's gone beyond that now.

And here's the weird thing. I'm not sorry. I don't feel guilty. I mean, maybe I do a little, or I wouldn't be writing this, I guess. But Frank would never understand the feelings Mr. Stevenson has somehow awakened in me, or planted in me, or whatever he's done. And Mrs. Stevenson—I guess she isn't really real to me. Perhaps she is his Madonna and I am his whore. Perhaps between us we give him what he needs.

Each day for the past week I've worn the pretty panties he bought for me, and each day, though he's found a reason to use his ruler, or embarrass me in some delicious way, he had yet to see what he'd purchased. Did I expect him to ask me to model it as Miss Reynolds had?

Yes, to be honest, I guess I did. You don't buy a woman sexy underwear like that and then not want to see it, do you? If you're a normal red-blooded man, that is. I guess that's my mistake. While I find Mr. Stevenson exciting and even dangerous in a sexy kind of way, I certainly wouldn't describe him as warm.

But I'm digressing. Let me get on with this and maybe then its power over me won't be so strong. Mr. Stevenson called me in after lunch. He wasn't hunched over his papers as usual, but was sitting in one of his wing-backed visitor's chairs, looking casual and quite handsome without his suit jacket on.

"I presume you're wearing the panties and garters I expect you to wear daily?"

"Yes, Sir," I said, suddenly finding the air in the room to be short of oxygen.

"I'd like to see for myself." For a minute I misunderstood, thinking he meant for me to go get the little pile of satin and lace I keep in a hatbox under the sink in the office bathroom. I almost turned to go and get it like a dope, but he clarified, "Take off your dress, please. Your slip too. Now." He smiled, softening that stern gaze he has.

I reached back to unzip my dress. After all, I had stopped wearing my girdle and cotton underpants while at work, and though he's never said a word of praise about my figure, I have found lately that I feel sexy and attractive, knowing I am wearing this lovely finery beneath my practical secretary's wardrobe.

I stepped out of my dress and slip, draping them over the arm of the couch. I stood there, this time determined not to betray my nervousness as I had the last time he'd seen me in my undies.

Mr. Stevenson looked me over, his eyes raking me so that I felt the blush start in my cheeks and work its way down. "Very nice. Miss Reynolds has an eye for what works, doesn't she?" I didn't answer, not sure what to say. He went on, "You look beautiful, Olivia." Finally! I bit back a grin. So, the man was human!

Slowly he stood and walked toward me. I could smell his cologne—something spicy but subtle, and I could smell the faint scent of starch on his fine tailored shirt. I think I was actually trembling when he leaned over, bringing his face close.

Very lightly, almost tentatively, he brought his mouth to mine. I stood very still, not quite sure even as it was happening that he was kissing me. But that's what it was. He gave me a kiss. A chaste, closed-mouth kiss, but a kiss nonetheless. Then he brought his arms around me and let his hands rest on my bottom! I felt his fingers smoothing the fine silk fabric of the panties he'd paid for. I shivered, wanting to press into him, wanting to feel his mouth on mine again.

And yet, I didn't move. Somehow, I knew I wasn't supposed to respond as a lover would. I wasn't supposed to kiss him back, to wrap my own arms around him, to pull him down with me to the floor.

No, I was to stand there, passive and obedient, while his hands roamed my body, moving from my bottom up my back, back down to my thighs. Finally, he stood away from me, putting his palm flat against my sex. I could feel the heat of his hand against the panties, and I felt this kind of burning desire inside that I don't recall feeling since Frank and I used to grope each other when we'd go "parking" before we were married.

I could feel my heart rattling around in my rib cage as we locked eyes. His fingers moved down between my legs, though still over the panties. I felt dizzy. On the one hand, I could hardly believe this was happening, but on the other, what had all these days and weeks been leading up to? Surely, we both knew it was going to move into something overtly sexual. How could it be otherwise?

"Take off your panties please, Olivia." Thinking back on it now, it's odd that he asked me to take off my panties, before asking me to take off my bra. You'd think he'd want to see my breasts first, wouldn't you? But he didn't. No, he sat down again, with me still standing there trembling and blushing, as he repeated, "Take off the panties. I want to see your pussy."

Pussy. Such a crude word! From such a refined man. I turned away and he said, his voice quiet but stern, "Olivia. Your modesty is charming, but most disobedient. I've made a simple request. It's not a demand. You may refuse. I've enjoyed our developing relationship, but certainly we're under no compulsion to continue. You've done an admirable job as my legal secretary and if that's all you wish to remain, I'll be happy to provide two weeks salary and whatever references you need to procure a similar post. Do I make myself clear?"

He did. Crystal clear. Strip or you're fired. That was the bottom line, wasn't it? And yet, why should I take offense? I'd gone along inch-by-inch with him as we've taken each bizarre and dangerous step in this peculiar dance in which we're engaged. Certainly, I would look ridiculous suddenly taking umbrage because he wanted to move forward in the game. And truth to tell, I wanted to also.

It's just that the "modesty" he referred to, charming or otherwise, wasn't false. My God, no one except Dr. Morrison has seen my privates, other than Frank, of course, who I don't think has actually looked at me naked since before Frank Jr. was born. Now this man, my boss, my potential lover, was calmly asking me to pull down my panties so he could see my "pussy".

Feeling wildly reckless, spurred on no doubt by my own arousal, I did it. I peeled my panties down, keeping my eyes locked on his as I kicked them aside. I stood there, my face as hot as a fever, crossing my hands in front of my sex, determined not to grab my clothes and run out of that office, determined to stand my ground and see what came next.

He stood again, his eyes smoldering, dark but kind of sparkly. He really is quite a good-looking man. He approached me again, and this time when his lips touched mine, they were parted and I felt his tongue against my lips. I kissed him back. This time we shared a lover's kiss.

His arms went around me again and I felt him unclasping my bra. I kept on kissing him, feeling like we were in high school, like if I didn't acknowledge what was happening it wouldn't count. He let the bra fall between us as I pushed close against him, shy about his seeing my breasts.

He held me and I felt his erection against my belly. Then I felt his hand on my sex again, and his fingers pressed against my cleft. My impulse was to push him away. What was he doing! But then his fingers grazed across my sex, pressing down, drawing wetness from me. My God, I've never felt anything like it.

His fingers were...oh, I don't even have words for it. It was like this warm, lovely buttery feeling, spreading from his fingertips up through me, making me feel weak in the knees. I like sex. I mean, I never really understood what all the hoopla was about, but I liked it well enough. Especially after a few glasses of champagne. But this was different.

Sex with Frank, my one and only, is always about Frank. I mean, I know that's normal and all, as men have that high sex drive and what have you, but Frank certainly never touched me the way Mr. Stevenson did! When he touched me so intimately, a part of me thought this is dirty, this is wrong. But you know what? I don't really believe that. What's wrong about feeling such pleasure?

Well, I wasn't thinking any of that stuff right then, I can tell you. I wasn't thinking at all. I was feeling. Feeling his fingers, at once soft as butterfly wings, yet as firm and insistent as all of Mr. Stevenson's actions. I sighed and sort of sagged there in his arms, wishing I could lie down, or at least take off my shoes.

I think he took pity on me because he led me to the couch and kind of pushed me down into a sitting position. He knelt between my legs, himself still fully clothed. I was just in my garters, stockings and shoes, like a French whore, with him kneeling between my legs, his fingers now buried in my sex.

Again, instead of screaming with outrage, I was moaning with pure unadulterated lust. It felt so good! I think I could have climaxed if he hadn't stopped. I didn't want him to stop, but he did and I didn't have the nerve to ask him to go on. But I wanted it. I wanted it in the worst way.

Is this normal? Am I turning into some kind of crazy nymphomaniac? I wish I could talk to someone about this! Another woman. A friend. God, can you imagine Betty's face if I tried to tell her any of this? The shock! The outrage! The disbelief!

And it isn't only that my boss and I are having an affair, because I can't deny that now, even though we haven't "done the deed" as Frank would say. It's so much more. Mr. Stevenson is so different from Frank. They're like night and day. Where I give in to Frank, I do it because it's my wifely duty. That sounds corny maybe, but that's how I was raised, I guess.

But with Mr. Stevenson, oh with him, the submission, if that's what you call it, is as much for me as for him. Maybe more. This burning intensity, this heightened feeling—it's beyond words for me. He has awoken something in me. Something I didn't know I possessed, didn't know I needed.

That's it!

I need what he offers. I want to submit to him. I want what he's giving. I need it.

I'm scared.

_*_

"I want you to read this." Brad stepped into Tess's office at their law firm. It was four o'clock, nearing the end of a long day. Tess looked up from her work and smiled, surprised to see her lover in the middle of the day. They had kept their affair quiet at the office, knowing it would be out soon enough, cherishing their privacy while it lasted.

Brad approached her, looking handsome and professional, with his unruly hair forced back with gel and his silk tie neatly knotted below his Adam's apple. He handed her a small book wrapped in brown paper. Their fingers touched as she took the gift and even there, in the formal setting of her office, she felt an electric spark between them and a moistening between her legs.

"See you tonight," he said softly before leaving her alone with the package. Tess opened it slowly, curious what he had given to her. After they had made love the night before, they'd gone on to read the rest of the journal entry about Olivia's adventure in the high-fashion clothing store. The woman described as Miss Reynolds had inspected a blushing Olivia, touching her in a rather familiar manner as she adjusted the panties just so and had Olivia turn and model for her in her underwear. Tess found herself forgetting that Olivia and Nana were one and the same. Olivia was instead becoming a friend, admittedly from another time, but someone she would like to know. Not as her grandmother, but as a person.

Last night after Brad had fallen asleep Tess had lain awake, musing on Brad's words and what he seemed to be asking of her. Clearly, he was as turned on as she, if not more so, by the submissive nature of the developing relationship between Olivia and Mr. Stevenson.

And his talk of control. Of controlling her. She understood that he didn't mean it in the traditional sense, that is, he didn't want to order her around, make decisions for her about her professional life or her financial affairs or anything like that. No, she understood instinctively that he was talking about something different. Something like that which was developing between the secretary and her boss, on parallel lines forty years in the past.

Something sexual, but more than that. Something more intense and vital than mere sexual dominance. Tess was intrigued, deeply intrigued, and more obsessed about Brad than ever. One thing she knew for certain—she had never had such intense orgasms with another man. Brad knew how to touch her, how to speak to her, even how to look at her, in a way that set her blood on fire.

She unwrapped the book and looked at its cover. It was a very simple cover, all white with the black print discreetly placed in a rectangle in the center. She read the words, *Charlotte's Awakening* by Paulette Rouge.

Opening the slim volume, she began to read, her legal brief forgotten...

The reception area was dark and most of the support staff had gone home. Many of the attorneys were still in their offices, and Tess was no exception. Only she wasn't working. She had shut her door and asked her secretary to hold all but emergency calls for the remainder of the day. She'd done enough billable hours that week to allow herself these few hours without guilt.

She hadn't planned on reading the entire book in one sitting, but once she had started, she couldn't put it down. It was an erotic, sexually explicit story, not something Tess was used to reading. Charlotte, a young woman in turn of the century England, takes a lover who forces his dominant will upon her, teaching her to submit in every aspect of her life. It was erotic, but not especially romantic, as the lover Sir Jonathan seemed strangely cold and forbidding. Charlotte's descent into complete submission and subjugation at the hands of her lover, and at the hand of the men he chose to share her with made Tess's face burn, but her pussy throb.

Intellectually, Tess rebelled as she read it. What was wrong with this woman, allowing herself to be used and debased? Not only allowing herself, but seeking it, craving it? And yet, again, hearing the whisper of the secret language underlying the tale, Tess's body responded with an intensity that shocked her. Her palms were sweating and she felt almost dizzy as the story unfolded. Her nipples stirred with electric desire as the descriptions of forced sex and whippings pulled a response from her. Her panties were soaked and a strange sort of fever had fallen over her. Luckily, no one had disturbed her as she read.

Finally closing the book, she sat back, feeling as if she'd just run a race. The ending was upsetting, with Charlotte's lover ultimately abandoning her for a younger woman when he was "done" with her. The final scene, with Charlotte bent over her needlework by an insufficient coal fire in the tiny room to which she had been relegated, was heartbreaking. Overall, Tess decided that she didn't like the book. But the sensual and submissive ideas in it had gripped her utterly.

And the fact that Brad had given it to her. Brad had wanted her to read this. He had shown her more with this book than hours and hours of conversation and discussion.

Did he want to be her Sir Jonathan? No, Tess knew Brad, unlike the caricature of a Dom in the story, was romantic and that love was definitely part of their equation. And yet, the images and ideas portrayed in the story had captivated her.

Her thoughts turned to Nana, to Olivia and her diaries. Had she read this book? Tess opened the fly page, looking for a copyright. 1954. So, it was out when Olivia had begun her own submissive journey. No, Tess seriously doubted if Olivia would ever have had the opportunity to come across a book like this.

At first, Tess had wanted to continue to devour the journals, reading as much as possible in one fell swoop. But Brad's gentle insistence that they just read a bit at a time had turned out to be a strange but exciting addition to their own love life. It was as if they were developing along their own parallel path of D/s exploration. Each night was a new adventure as they read the latest installment in the secret diaries.

How amazing, Tess thought, that she and her grandmother shared this submissive tendency and yet neither of them had been aware of it until a man had entered their life and held out a promise of something different, something dangerous but compelling.

Certainly, Nana had never shared it with Tess, even during their heart-to-hearts when Tess was in college. She realized now, thinking back, that the focus had always been on her—on Tess's dreams and ideas, Tess's longings and questions. Nana had shared stories about her past, of course, but there was never the slightest hint of any secret life.

Tess's phone rang. It was an interoffice line. Brad. She picked up, saying automatically, "Tess Shepard."

"It's after seven. What're you still doing here?"

"I could ask you the same thing, counselor," she retorted.

"Well, I'm packing it in. How about you? Wanna get something to eat?"

"Sure." Not a word about the book, but then she hadn't brought it up either. In a moment, Brad's handsome head was poking around her door and they left together, the little white book tucked into Tess's briefcase.

The restaurant was packed, forcing Tess and Brad to wait at the bar for a table. They came in one car, deciding they'd get Tess's from the law office parking lot later.

"You read the book."

It wasn't a question. Tess nodded, feeling a curious heat in her face. Why should she be embarrassed? Surely, they were beyond that.

On the way in the car, Brad had made a curious request. "Take off your pantyhose." Tess had giggled, assuming he wanted to fondle her, and that was fine with her. She enjoyed his hands on her legs, sometimes straying higher, teasing her with promises of what would come later in the bedroom. After squirming out of the nylons, she slipped her pumps back onto bare feet and looked over at him.

"Now what?" she asked grinning, feeling a sweet heat in her pussy in anticipation of his attentions. But he didn't touch her. He had barely seemed to notice as she had lifted her bottom, pulling the confining mesh from her body, revealing her firm, tan legs. He remained focused on the road. Tess sighed but didn't want to seem too needy and so she too stared ahead, watching the headlights of the oncoming cars, vignettes from *Charlotte's Awakening* drifting into her mind.

Now sitting at the restaurant's bar, Brad said, "Take off your panties. Sit your bare ass on the stool, like Charlotte did."

Tess turned to him in surprise, but Brad didn't meet her eye. He continued staring at the bar, his beer mug in his hand. Tess felt a flutter in her chest. She looked around the crowded room. People were pressed in all around them.

"Here?"

"Yes. Do it right there. No one will notice. Just slip them down and tuck them into your purse. Make sure your bare ass is on that stool."

"Oh, Brad. That's crazy. I—"

"Tess. Do it." Something in his tone compelled her to obey. Glancing around nervously, Tess discreetly slid her fingers beneath her skirt. Lifting her bottom, she wriggled forward, edging the panties down bare thighs, slipping them down past her ankles. Bunching them into her fist, she shoved them in her purse. Pulling the fabric of her skirt, she let it fall over the back of the stool so that she was naked against it. She glanced around nervously but, as Brad had predicted, no one seemed to notice her.

The leather of the stool felt cold against her bare skin. The heat in her pussy made her shift, sliding her eyes toward Brad again. He turned slowly toward her, a smile curling on his face. Leaning over her, he kissed her lightly on the lips.

"Lovely," he murmured. "That's how I want you from now on, my darling. Bare-assed and available."

Tess flushed, feeling confused, even angry. Yet, if she were honest she couldn't deny the tug at her sex that his words evoked and the sweet hot wetness growing between her legs.

Their table was ready and Brad guided her gently by her elbow into the main dining room, pulling her chair out and nodding as she lifted the skirt and again sat so her bare skin touched the seat. Tess looked down at the table feeling shy and vulnerable but more aroused than she could ever remember. Brad had a way of making her burn. She loved the heat seeping from her pussy like liquid lust.

Brad was looking at the menu, pretending an indifference she was certain he couldn't be feeling. Surely, he was as aroused as she by their secret game here in public. After the waiter took their order Brad said, "Are you wet, Tess?"

"Um," she hedged, licking her lips.

"Touch yourself and tell me." Their eyes met and she saw the smoldering lust in his. Watching him, she reached beneath the table and under her skirt, letting her legs fall apart. She touched her swollen labia, surprised to find just how wet she was! Her own finger sent an electric jolt of pleasure through her body and she shuddered.

"Tell me," he said again, his voice soft and low.

"Yes," she whispered.

"Touch yourself. Do it for me." She didn't need to be asked twice. The pent-up arousal from reading the sadomasochistic tale of Charlotte, and then Brad's sexy dominance of her so far this evening had already sent Tess very close to the edge. Delicately, she let two fingers move together over her swollen sex, pulling up the wetness. Sighing quietly, she let her eyes flutter shut.

It felt wonderful and even though she was afraid someone might be aware of what she was doing, Tess felt herself moving quickly toward an intense orgasm at her own fingers.

"Stop." Dimly Tess heard Brad's command, but she continued to touch herself, too close now to stop. "Tess," his voice was more urgent, but still Tess ignored him, swaying on the edge of a glorious cliff of shattering pleasure. She plunged over, slamming her legs together, rocking herself to a sweet release with a low, husky moan.

When she opened her eyes, Brad was looking at her with a bemused smile and the waiter who had brought their drinks was gaping at her openmouthed, frozen in surprise. Tess gasped and sat upright, grabbing her napkin. She hid her face with it in her humiliation.

"Are those for us?" Brad inquired, pointing to the drinks the waiter still clutched in his hands, smiling at him as if nothing were amiss. The young man stammered and nodded, setting the drinks down with a clatter on the table. With a last glance at them, he scurried away.

Brad burst out laughing. "Now you see, Tess? Next time when I tell you to stop, you'd better obey!" Tess leaned over the table and punched him on the arm, but she was laughing too, despite her embarrassment. The expression on that poor waiter's face had been priceless and the erection in his pants had been testament to his opinion of her little display.

chapter 6

November 13, 1961

MR. STEVENSON IS the second man I've ever been intimate
with. God, listen to me. "Intimate with." Speak plainly,
Livvie! He's the second man I've had sex with. Fucked. The
word looks harsh to me. I don't like it. I prefer "making
love". Is that what we did? I really couldn't tell you. I do
know that that "final act" was not the main thing—not
the defining event of the evening. Not for me, anyway.

Maybe if I write this all down it will become clearer
as I go. Reveal itself to me, because right now I'm muddled.

How did this happen? Why don't I feel guiltier about
Frank? Truth to tell, I feel guiltier about the kids than
Frank! I've never been away from them ever, not one day
since Frank Jr. was born. This business trip thing was so
unexpected. To tell you the truth, I didn't think Frank
would go for it. I warned Mr. Stevenson that I would probably be unavailable. He assured me that he completely
understood, but that my services at his very important
meeting out of town would be invaluable and that of course

he would compensate me amply for my extra time—for the inconvenience of having to sleep away from my home.

I think that's what motivated Frank, to be brutally honest. I could earn in two days what I usually make in a week! He's had his eye on a new Buick and this would be just the ticket for the down payment. I know how to play Frank, I'm not ashamed to admit, and by acting very low-key and hesitant—as if I didn't really want to do this, and what about the children—I manipulated him into feeling he was the one advocating for the trip and I was the reluctant one.

"We'll be fine!" he assured me, grinning at the kids. "Won't we, kids? We can make it on our own for one night without Mom, can't we?" The kids nodded, and that's when I felt a gut-wrenching guilt. I was leaving my babies for two days and a night!

On the other hand, they would be with Frank, and as unsatisfying as he might be at times as a partner, I have to admit he's a good dad. They certainly wouldn't starve or be at any kind of risk. Promises of souvenirs from my trip brightened the kids considerably.

At any rate, I seem to be avoiding the task at hand, which is to put down what happened. What "transpired" as Mr. Stevenson is fond of saying in his legal opinions.

It's funny how I always refer to him as Mr. Stevenson. Here in this journal and even in my head, he is always Mr. Stevenson, even though I know his given name is James. Does his wife call him James, or something more endearing, like Jim or Jimmy? I can't see him as a Jimmy. I doubt he would tolerate nicknames. Not proper Mr. Stevenson.

Okay, okay, I'm going to write it. I have to write it. I have to "expunge" the record. But that won't happen, will it? I can't will it away by writing it down. What's happened has happened and there's no going back. Nor, if I am honest—and if I can't be honest here, what have I left?—do I want to.

During the day, the trip was actually legitimate, as I was to assist Mr. Stevenson in meetings with very important clients, acting as recorder and supplying all the needed documents and papers we'd spent the past month pulling together. I felt very professional and important in my new dress, and I also felt sexy and alive underneath, in my silken garters and lacy panties.

It was a long day full of smoky boardrooms and lots of dull fellows signing lots of papers. When it was finally over, we all shook hands. They even shook hands with me, even though I'm just a secretary. Then they went their way and we went ours. Which was to a very fine hotel, the Hallmark, five-star and very posh. I had my own room, of course, but it attached to Mr. Stevenson's by a thick door locked between us.

He had the key.

Over drinks in the hotel bar, Mr. Stevenson loosened up a bit. We weren't in our usual formal work environment, which made a difference I suppose. He asked me what I'd like and I said a Cosmopolitan, because I saw another woman get one and it looked good and I liked the shape of the glass. He nodded and ordered me one, along with a martini for himself, two olives on the side.

We made small talk and he complimented me on my work during the meetings, which made me feel all warm and happy. He ordered us a second round and I was feeling it already, as we hadn't even had dinner yet. He put his hand on mine and said quietly, "Are you ready, Olivia? Ready for the next step between us?"

Ready? Could a person be ready for this? Part of me felt more than ready. He looked so good without his tie on, his shirt unbuttoned two buttons so I could see a little patch of curly chest hair peeping out over his undershirt. His face looked relaxed and happy. He had, after all, just clinched a deal, where his representation of these particular clients should guarantee a steady and sizable cash flow for several years to come. But I wanted to think it was more than that.

I wanted to believe that he was happy and excited to be with me. I guess I felt as ready as I'd ever be, though I really didn't know what I was supposed to be ready for. I was pretty sure it involved us committing adultery and while I did feel guilty and not a little nervous, that second Cosmopolitan went down rather easily. I smiled at him, trying to appear calm and collected.

"I think so, Mr. Stevenson."

Another man at that point in the affair would surely have said, "Please, call me James." But he didn't. But this is hardly a typical "affair". Instead, he said, "Tonight is our chance to find out if you are truly submissive. I want to take you beyond limits you may think you have. I want to know that you are willing. And if you're not, believe me, that's fine. I have no intention of coercing you into any sort of behavior tonight. This isn't about our little punishment system at work, which, while amusing, is of course more of a game than anything.

"No, tonight I want to take you, us, further. We've talked about it before—my dominant bent and your submissive one. I want to find out if our connection goes beyond a mere predilection. Do you want that too, Olivia?"

Was it the liquor that made me so bold? Or his rather bald admission that he had needs and desires when it came to our relationship? Some combination of both, I expect. Anyway, tongue loosened, I answered, "Mr. Stevenson, I think I want it. But to tell you the truth, I don't really know what to expect. You talk in circles. You're indirect." I took another slug of the drink and said recklessly, "Just what is it you want? What do you expect from me?"

"It's a fair question," he said, actually grinning at me. "And a direct one. So, I'll be direct with you. You excite me. You're beautiful and sexy. More than that, I've come to value our relationship, aside from our professional one, of course, which is also highly satisfactory. What I'm trying to say is that I want you, Olivia.

"Not just for a romp in the sheets. I feel somehow you and I are destined for far more than that. Do you know how rare it is to find this kindred connection? No, of course you don't. Why would you? We have the chance, Olivia, you and me, to find out what we're made of together. You will have the chance to submit and I will have the chance to dominate, in a sensual sense, a woman who was born to it."

This gave me a clue, a definite clue, that he doesn't have the chance to "dominate" at least not in a sexual sense, elsewhere. So dear Mrs. Stevenson is as clueless to his "predilections" as he calls them, as Frank is to mine. How could it be otherwise, I suppose. Who would dare share these aberrant feelings without risk of destroying a marriage?

Of course, I wasn't thinking all this as he spoke. I was feeling a little giddy from the vodka and not a little nervous at the prospect of what was surely about to happen.

He called over the waitress and told her his room number and to put the drinks on his tab. Then we went up in the large quiet elevator—no operator, too modern—to our rooms. I was glad he didn't suggest dinner—there was no way I could have eaten anything at that point.

He unlocked my door for me and said, "I want you to get ready for me, Olivia. We've come to a new level in our relationship and I feel you are ready for the next step. I appreciate that you are, uh, new to this lifestyle and have certain reservations.

"I want to assure you that I have no plan to destroy your family or make any demands on you outside of the time we have together. This isn't about love—it's about something loftier."

This isn't about love. So, what's it about? But I'm being unfair. I know it isn't about love. Not precisely. Not schoolgirl romance ideas of love, at any rate. And I also appreciate that he was sending me his own message—that I better not go "falling in love" and messing up his perfect professional image, with his fine neighborhood, his country club, social paragon type lifestyle, his happy marriage either. Not that I have any designs to that effect. Frankly, I can admit here that our agendas are the same or at least the same in terms of what we don't want.

I didn't say any of that to him. Not a word. I just nodded at him and he went on talking, apparently satisfied. "I want you to strip to your underclothes. No slip. I want you to kneel on the floor, with your head touching the carpet. I want you to wait for me. I won't be long. I expect to find you in that position, absolutely still. You will not speak or move when you hear me enter. I expect absolute obedience. Do you understand?"

I felt dizzy and wished I hadn't had so much to drink. Kneel in my bra and panties, with my head on the carpet? Was the man insane? My usual voices piped up in my head, trying to pretend outrage, but I think the liquor pushed down my internal attempts to censor my real feelings.

I *felt* his command more than heard it. And I wanted it. I wanted to kneel on the ground like some kind of sex slave in those trashy novels at the drugstore. The ones I never buy but just stand there thumbing through while the pharmacist glares at me.

He shut my door, leaving me alone in my lovely room. The bed had been turned down and there was a fancy little chocolate wrapped in gold set in the center of a plump pillow, a pretty scrolled "H" pressed into the foil.

Carefully, I removed my clothing, including the slip. I glanced in the mirror, brushed my hair a little, applied fresh lipstick, took a big breath, asked myself out loud what the heck I was doing and knelt on the ground.

Perhaps five minutes passed. It certainly seemed longer, but I still had my wristwatch on and it was only about five. I heard the snick of the key in the lock of the adjoining door. He came in quietly, his steps muffled by the soft, thick carpet. I felt his hand on my back for a moment, and then I saw his shoes in front of me. I started to rise but felt his hand again on my back and I stayed down.

My heart was thumping so loud I expect he could hear it. "Olivia. For the rest of the night you belong to me. To use as I see fit, in any way I choose. If you accept these terms, stay kneeling. If not, get up now and I'll go back to my room and we'll have dinner downstairs and that will be that. We can still go on as before in the office. This is not an ultimatum. I don't want you unless you're ready to give yourself to me."

I stayed down, though now my heart seemed to be up somewhere in my throat. What a picture I must have presented—a grown woman in her underwear, granted it was sexy underwear but still, kneeling there half-naked with my boss, waiting for him to tell me just exactly what to do! No one in the PTA would ever imagine...

I felt him pulling me up and I let him. We were standing now face-to-face, though without my shoes, I only came up to his chest. He wrapped me in those strong arms and bent down, kissing me like any lover. His hands were roaming over my back and bottom and I responded, pressing into him, wrapping my own arms around him.

After a few moments, he pulled away and murmured, "For tonight, you are to call me 'Master'." He looked at me, his expression intense. "And to me you will be 'slave'. No names tonight, not even surnames. Do you understand?"

I nodded, though I confess that I thought this was rather silly. Master, slave—like something out of Scheherazade. And yet, I found myself responding, as I always seem to, to his direct command. The Master and his slave girl. What a fantasy! And the fantasy was becoming reality. It felt more real than anything I've ever experienced. I don't know how to convey it, but when we descend—or ascend?—into these roles, this Master and slave thing, my whole realm of experience seems heightened somehow. Colors are brighter, sensations more vivid. I feel more alive somehow, as if the rest of my life is shadow and black and white and only this is the real thing.

He took off the rest of my clothing, though I don't specifically recall him doing it. He was kissing me the whole time. He still remained fully clothed himself and now he said, "Have you ever been whipped, slave?"

I stared at him and he smiled. "No, of course not," he answered for me. "And now in your mind, you see it as some kind of Marquis de Sade torture. But it isn't. It isn't when it's done right, as a loving act. I'm going to show you, darling. I'm going to introduce you to something you've never dreamed about. Now lie down on your stomach, just relax." He pointed to the bed. "I'll be right back."

Darling! He'd called me "darling". Believe it or not, that's what I focused on during his talk of whips and torture. I dutifully lay down on the bed, not quite so foggy now from liquor, as adrenaline shot through me. I lay there wondering what the heck I was getting myself into, but knowing I was going to go through with it.

He came back and I looked over at him. He had taken off his shirt and his torso was strong and firm. I felt guilty comparing, but immediately Frank's flabby chest and pot-belly popped into my mind's eye. Then I was distracted by what he was holding—a long, black whip, all shiny leather and soft suede. I gasped and sat up, clutching myself protectively.

He was next to me in a flash, sitting on the bed, soothing me with his words and hands. "Shh, don't worry, slave. This will only happen at your pace. You will call the shots. You will ask me for the whip when you're ready. Until then, let me show you how sensual it can be." He pressed me back down onto my tummy and soothed me with soft words. His touch was so gentle, so sensual, so at odds with the stern man from the office.

And yet, not really. Just another facet, I suppose, of a complicated man. I relaxed and closed my eyes, enjoying the sensation of being naked on soft sheets and having someone touch and smooth my body. Eventually, I realized it was no longer his hand on my flesh, but the soft tresses of the whip gliding up and down my back, bottom and thighs. And he was right—it was soft, sensual—lovely, really.

And what would it feel like if he were to raise the whip and let the tresses fall harder against the flesh? Just a little bit? I licked my lips, wondering if I should ask or just see what he would do. He continued to run the leather up and down my body until my skin was tingling and ready somehow for something more. I found myself asking, as he had said I would, "Please. Perhaps a little harder?" He complied, lifting the whip so that the tresses fell against my bottom, just hard enough to make their presence felt.

I found it didn't hurt at all, but created a lovely hot sensation inside of me. He did it several more times, still light enough to barely register as more than a gentle sting. "Spread your legs, slave," he commanded, and I did, feeling lewd but incredibly sexy, knowing he could see my bared sex if he leaned down.

I felt his hand on me and he whispered, "You're soaking, slave. You need this, don't you? You need more than I'm giving you now, don't you?"

I did. God, I'm admitting it here, though I don't understand it, but yes, I did. I nodded and he said, "Then ask for it. Ask me to whip you harder. To make you wetter." His fingers swirled over me and one pressed its way into me, and I shuddered and resisted the urge to hump his hand!

Me!

"Please, Master," I said, the word sliding out of my mouth like it had always been under my tongue. "Whip me harder." I clenched my body, suddenly afraid.

The whip came down and this time it really stung! *Ouch!* I jerked under the lash and he did it again. Here's the weird thing! It did hurt. It stung up and down my back and bottom, and yet, and yet...I didn't want it to stop. The pain mingled with the pleasure in my sex and, I actually moaned out loud.

"Yes," he whispered, and instead of stopping and taking me in his arms, he continued to whip me harder and harder until I was wriggling around, my skin on fire, a passion boiling in my blood. God. Frank wouldn't have recognized me. I rolled over suddenly and his whip landed on my belly and breast. That really hurt, like the sharp sting of a bee on my nipple. I squealed, the pleasure receding.

He dropped the whip then and kissed the nipple that a second before had been struck with his whip. I know he didn't mean to do that. I was the one who had rolled over unexpectedly. The feel of his mouth on my body erased the sting and I forgot my "place" as his "slave" and just pulled him down onto me, seeking his mouth, those lips, with mine.

The actual act—when he entered me, well, to tell you the truth, it wasn't much different than with Frank. Except he had to use one of those nasty rubber things. Of course, I was glad and relieved he did for obvious reasons, but I've never liked them.

Listen to me! I just reread what I wrote and I can't believe it's my pen writing these words. I gave in to sex with a man who is not my husband so I could get whipped? How bizarre is that? I can't believe it's me, but I'm not going to sit here and pretend it didn't happen.

I want what he offers. I want more than he's offered so far. Now the question is, how am I going to get it?

chapter 7

"Wow," Tess murmured. She and Brad were lying naked in her bed, reading together that latest fiery entry. "She got whipped. Whipped, Brad! Can you imagine?"

Tess's incredulity was partially feigned. She herself could imagine it well, and had. But only in her dreams. There was a dream, a particular dream that had haunted her ever since she had read Charlotte's story.

"Can't you, Tess?"

Tess swallowed, the images of her dream still marking her mind's eye.

To be whipped.

It was one thing to read about it in some erotica novel or even in another woman's journal, written forty years before. In her dream, Tess was naked, bound with thick rope at ankle and wrist, held in a cruciform position by her bonds. The sweat was gleaming on her pale, taut body. She could see herself from all angles, as if she were the one who held the whip. Yes, the whip.

A tall man stood near her. She couldn't see his face and he didn't say a word. She could feel his power. A sensual power but also a dangerous power. Something she couldn't control. She was spread wide, naked and vulnerable, as he stood just behind her, out of her sight, his face obscured in the shadows. He held a whip, but he hadn't whipped her—not yet.

She could hear her own breathing. She could feel the sweat on her body, on her face, tickling her underarms. She was fiercely aroused. She knew the man was looking at her, appraising her naked form, possibly finding fault. A mixture of shame and desire slid through her. Above it all, she wanted the whip. She wanted to feel it cut her flesh. The desire was intensely sexual and this man was clearly her lover. His whip would make love to her. And yet, when he raised the whip, to strike her, to mark her, to claim her, she would wake up, trembling and alone.

Brad was watching her. Softly he said, "Tell me what you're thinking."

"I'm having this flash of a daydream I guess," she said. "Actually, it's a dream I had. I've had it a few times, really." She flushed and stopped, embarrassed.

"Tell me."

How to describe the hot tension of the dream? The danger, the excitement, the unrealized lust. It was so hard to capture the essence of a dream. She didn't try. She only gave him the barest outline of the images, leaving out the secret feelings of need, mingled with shame, as yet unexplored.

"Me. Standing up in a room, my wrists and ankles bound with rope. And someone behind me holding a big whip. I can't see him but I know he has a whip. The whole room is in shadow and nothing has really happened yet.

But I know he's about to whip me. It's that tension—the tension that it's just about to happen, that makes it so intense, I think."

"Do you want that?" Brad kissed her eyelids shut. Speaking in a soft, seductive voice, he murmured, "You, tied and bound, helpless really. Out of control. No way out. The thick rope cutting into your wrists and ankles if you struggle against it. You feel your pussy—a slight breeze against its heat. You're turned on but scared. Who wouldn't be scared? You're going to be whipped! Flogged, with a big, dangerous whip. And there's no one there to set you free. To stop the stranger standing behind you, his face in shadow."

Brad's voice became more animated as he took over the images in her dream, embellishing them with his own imagination. "You would have to take it, Tess. To take the beating and afterwards, when he dropped the whip and let you down, maybe he'd fuck you. Fuck you from behind, still not allowing you to see his face. He would order you to push your cunt back, to open yourself for him. And you would do it, wouldn't you? Your ass would be burning from the whip but your pussy would be burning even more, wouldn't it, slut? Because you know you want it. You need it. You long to feel the kiss of a whip and the thrust of a man's hard cock."

Tess opened her eyes, staring at the man who'd just articulated her secret fantasies better than she ever could have. Was he himself offering this? Or was it just a game—a way to turn her on before he made love to her?

She dared ask, her voice coming out in a husky whisper, "Is that what you want, Brad? Would that excite you?

To whip a woman and then fuck her like that?" *To whip me*, she hadn't said, but had meant. She was still feeling her way in her own heart about all this. How astounding that he seemed to instinctively understand it all and be able to say it so freely!

Brad smiled at her, his eyes bright. He licked his lower lip, his eyes locked on hers. "Tess. I haven't ever whipped a woman. I don't own a whip—not yet." Tess took a little breath, noting the use of the word "yet" and all that it implied.

He continued. "Here's what I think. I think you and I are both interested in this. No, that's not the right word. We both want it but we're still feeling our way. I think somehow with this diary you've stumbled onto something that is, I don't know, kind of giving us permission to explore it ourselves, on our own terms."

He went on, warming to the topic. "This journal, it's in the past. This already happened a long time ago. And *Charlotte's Awakening*, that story was told a long time ago too. But we're here now. In this modern age where expressing yourself sexually, as long as it's consensual and doesn't harm anyone, is supposed to be cool.

"So bottom line, it isn't 'sick' or 'perverted' unless we think it is. I don't think it is. I think it's exciting, and sexy. I've never met a woman before where I felt safe enough to explore the whole idea of submission and sadomasochistic play, until I found you.

"Sure, I've tried some of the classic moves, like pinning my girlfriend in a playful wrestling match and then pretending to spank her, to see how she'd react. But it was never more than giggling and a game, which fizzled out or got weird if I tried to take it any further."

"You spanked girls?" Tess grinned, punching him playfully in the arm. But her bottom tingled with anticipation.

"You ever been spanked?" Brad asked, his expression serious.

Tess quieted and shook her head. "Not counting when I was a kid, you mean."

"No, not that. As a woman. As a part of sex. As foreplay." He pulled her to him, pressing her breasts against his chest. Bringing his hand down to her bare ass, he playfully swatted her.

Tess wriggled against him and said, "I haven't, of course. It's weird, because while it really turned me on to read all that stuff in *Charlotte's Awakening*, I don't know if I'd like it in real life. I mean, I'm not into pain. I stub my toe and I scream. So why does it thrill me so to read about a woman like Charlotte being chained and brutally whipped by her lover's butler, being raped by the chauffeur and casually sodomized by her lover?"

Brad thought a moment and answered, smiling a little, "Stubbing your toe has nothing to do with sensual submission and erotic pain. What I got out of the story was that it isn't the pain per se. It's the submission—the erotic submission. The idea of giving yourself over to someone else. And also, it's a heightened sensation, more than pain, that I think the submissive experiences. You know, I can't say directly, because my desires go along a parallel path, but not the same path, as yours. Let's see, your Nana's Mr. Stevenson summed it up, remember? Let's see."

Brad grabbed the journal that had fallen when they'd embraced. Thumbing through the pages until he found what he wanted, he read aloud, "'Do you know how rare it is to find this kindred connection? We have the chance to find out what we're made of together. You will have the chance to submit, and I will have the chance to dominate, in a sensual sense, a woman who was born to it.'

"That's it, isn't it? You and I have the same chance, Tess, if we choose to take it."

_*_

Tess noted that the diary entries were becoming slowly less ambivalent. It seemed Olivia had gotten past the initial period of doubt, confusion and guilt. She was now firmly in the middle of an all-out affair, though admittedly a most unusual one.

Tess found herself obsessed with Olivia. What must it have been like to go through this experience with so little direction or understanding—trusting only to her own instincts, and the constant pressure and control of her lover who was also her boss?

Tess decided that Mr. Stevenson must have been very like Sir Jonathan, though not as distant, surely. But his role was very much that of the traditional elusive "Master" who took what he wanted without revealing his own potential weakness or need.

Brad was more playful and fun, which suited Tess's own temperament better. Of course, their dynamic was different—they were lovers and equals, not boss and employee.

What would it have been like, to be working for someone, and have them slowly come to control all aspects of your behavior, at least for that set period of time you shared together each day?

After their "consummation" of the affair, things at Olivia's workplace became quite different, or not different precisely, but more radical. Now that they'd passed a certain point, Mr. Stevenson was clearly less hesitant to introduce his protégé to the increasingly bizarre demands and requirements of whatever game it was they were playing.

~*~

December 4, 1961
Where do I start? When did this change take place? I guess the line was crossed that evening we spent together. Of course, he didn't stay the night in my hotel room, and I suppose I was just as glad. It was a lot to process, having just betrayed my husband in a final and absolute sense. But if I'm really honest—which I try to be here, and yet even here I find myself censoring, and hedging...I really must stop that—I betrayed Frank the first time I let Mr. Stevenson use a ruler on my knuckle, or stare at me in that way he has, as if he can see not only my naked body through my clothing, but my very heart and soul.

And yet, at the same time I don't feel as if I've betrayed anyone. I am still the same Livvie at home, taking care of Frank and kids, involved in everyone's lives, behaving as I always do. If anything, guilt has driven me to be even more attentive to my husband. And as long as I keep it "ladylike"—I'm coming to realize how ridiculous this is, the limits we put on ourselves and let others put on us—Frank seems happy enough with our sex life.

I am reasonably able to compartmentalize my life, leaving my submissive behaviors and Mr. Stevenson's influence here at the office when I leave. And Mr. Stevenson has never asked me to do things after hours, for which I am grateful. Because while a part of me would thrill to it in a way, I appreciate, and I think he appreciates even more, that it wouldn't be a good idea. Better to keep what we have just where we have it.

And what do we have?

Perhaps I'll just write for a while. Tell some of the things we've begun to incorporate into our little world here in this office. My daily routine has changed somewhat. I still come in a half-hour before Mr. Stevenson and remove my girdle and practical underpants, replacing them with garters and pretty panties. I have a dozen pairs now, and I wash them out at the end of the day and leave them discreetly to dry overnight on a little rack I brought for the purpose.

But now, if we aren't expecting any clients, I am to remove my bra as well, but put back my dress or blouse and jacket. Sometimes, he'll take no notice of this the entire day, but I will be aware. Oh, my, will I! The feeling of the material against my bare breasts. My nipples becoming so sensitive. Sometimes I even go to the bathroom, just to touch and twist them. They have become "needy"—Mr. Stevenson's term.

He explains that he wants each part of my body to become needy, to experience a constant readiness and desire for his touch, whether it be gentle or harsh. He says we will focus on a different part each week, slowly sensitizing me to respond on his command.

We've begun with the breasts. Luckily, my breasts aren't too large. I was frankly worried about going without a bra, as certainly no grown woman would do that, especially not in an office! But then, I never dreamed I'd be working for someone like Mr. Stevenson and allowing the things that have happened to happen!

It's been a progression and each new step seems to follow in a way that feels right to me. I don't want to stop. I want to go further—to see where he'll take me and how far I'll be willing to go. He still wants me to write about what I'm feeling, to explore it honestly and without editing my reactions.

"Keep it honest, Olivia. This isn't for my consumption. It is for yours alone. Be honest with yourself. Sometimes that is harder than you think." He's right. Sometimes, I find myself wanting to deny my own feelings, or deny that something aroused me. Are there others out there like me? Is my behavior sick and twisted or just another facet of sexuality, as Mr. Stevenson staunchly claims?

Yesterday, he came to stand in front of my desk. I was just finishing a letter and I finished typing the sentence before looking up at him. "Unbutton your blouse." Keeping my eyes on his face, I obediently unbuttoned the top two buttons of my blouse. He nodded, indicating I should continue with all the buttons. My silly fingers were trembling. Even though he's now seen me completely naked, I still feel shy displaying myself like this!

I undid all the buttons, pulling the blouse from my skirt to get at the bottom buttons. Mr. Stevenson reached down and put his hand inside the open blouse, cupping a breast. His hand was cool and gentle against me, and I know he could feel the thudding of my heart. His fingers slid together, meeting at the nipple, which he rolled between them, gently at first, then with more pressure.

I felt my own response as my nipple hardened and distended in his hand. I felt heat in my face. It is so annoying the way I constantly blush! I wish I could control that, but Mr. Stevenson told me once that he likes it. He says he likes to elicit that response in me. He says he likes to know my blood is responding to him. I still hate it.

Anyway, he drew his hand away and my other breast felt "needy"—it wanted to be touched and teased too! He pulled the blouse apart, completely exposing me and I gripped the desk to resist my impulse to pull it shut again. At the same time, I felt the heat in my sex. His very blue eyes were bright and he whispered, "What do you want, Olivia?"

I didn't answer at first, and he asked again, more a demand than a question. Faltering a little, I admitted that I wanted him to touch the other breast. He smiled and did as I asked, this time twisting the nipple harder, making me cry out a little.

It hurt. It actually did, but I experienced the same thrill as when he caressed and whipped me with the leather flogger that night in the hotel. It wasn't the pain per se that thrilled me, that excited me. It was that he was doing it to me, his eyes smoldering and gleaming with something powerful.

"You know," he said casually, though I could see the erection in his fine tailored pants. "A good legal secretary needs excellent powers of concentration. Let's see how well you can concentrate, Olivia, while being distracted." He lifted a sheet of paper from a file on my desk and said, "Have you prepared these briefs yet?"

"No, Sir. You only just gave them to me this morning." He raised an eyebrow, and I realized my response might have sounded impertinent. I looked down, my eyes falling on my bare breasts, the nipples poking out, red like little cherries.

"All right then," he said. "I want you to begin with this one. Type up the comments I've made. Focus completely on your task, no matter what I do to you. Do you understand?" I nodded, biting back a grin. I love this kind of game, and I was hot-to-trot at that point. But then he said, "I'm going to inspect your work, Olivia. For each error I find, I will punish you. Is that clear?" The grin faded, replaced by a slight tremor of fear zipping through me.

Still I nodded, completely under his spell as always. I got out some heavy bond and slid it through my trusty typewriter, trying to act calm and professional, which is hard to do when your blouse is completely unbuttoned.

Mr. Stevenson came up behind me, and at first he just stood there. My fingers felt rubbery under his watchful eye. I was determined not to make a stupid typing error just because he was there. At first, I had no problem, but then I felt his hands on my shoulders. He pushed the blouse down so that it hampered my armse as I tried to type. I could either leave it that way or wriggle out of the blouse.

He hadn't said anything about taking it off, so I just gamely tried to type along. Meanwhile his hands moved lower, sliding down my chest to my breasts. He lifted each in his hands, finding my nipples again between index fingers and thumb.

It was so strange! To be fondled while trying to type a brief! I felt my nipples lengthen and engorge as he compressed and twisted them, making me gasp. I must have stopped typing because he said, "Olivia! Pay attention to what you're doing! You forget yourself." I realized my eyes were shut, and I opened them, trying to find my spot on the page of his neat, angular script.

Another savage twist and I cried out again, my hands falling from the keys. "Focus!" he commanded, his voice hard. I tried to continue, to find my place and get my fingers to cooperate. I did manage a few more lines, but I was so aroused, and confused by the sensations of heat and desire deep in my belly, juxtaposed with the twisting sting of heightened nerve endings at the tips of my breasts.

I couldn't seem to catch my breath and I was no longer even pretending to try to type. He pulled my head back and kissed me hard on the mouth. I love his smell. His cologne and his own natural scent. I actually felt at that moment that I wanted him to make love to me—to enter me. He hasn't done it since that one time at the hotel.

I wonder about that sometimes. The games we play are highly sexual, but neither of us orgasms, at least not in front of the other. And yet, I go around so aroused all day that I can hardly wait sometimes to get home to Frank. His gropings and thrustings are better than nothing!

Mr. Stevenson kissed me a while and it was heavenly, but then abruptly he pulled away and stood up, smoothing back his hair. "Straighten yourself up, Olivia. And meet me in my office. Bring your typing."

Oh, the errors! Typos right and left. He pretended to look grave, but I saw the twinkle in his eye. I stood in front of his desk, my blouse back on my shoulders, though I hadn't dared to button it up. I felt like a slut with my open blouse, smeared lipstick, mussed hair. I stood there, waiting for him to hand down the "punishment". I was expecting the usual choice—the ruler over the skirt or under, or a barehanded spanking over his knee. I pretend to hate it, but, oh, I love it.

He threw me for a total loop. I can't believe I'm going to write this. But here goes. Here were the options that day. "Olivia, I've sensed that you are coming to, ah, enjoy our little punishment sessions. Which really isn't surprising, as I had you pegged as a masochist from your first week here." I flushed, as usual, but also as usual, he was right on the money.

"Today we're going to try something different. The punishment will be more overtly sexual in nature, but I think you are at the point where you can handle it, slave." Don't think I didn't notice him calling me that! He hadn't called me that since the hotel, and I hadn't called him "Master" either. He went on, "Today you have a choice. You may either fellate me, or use your own hand to bring yourself to orgasm in front of me. And because I am aware of your suburban sensibilities, I know either option will indeed be a punishment, at least at this point in your sexual development."

Lord! The man can get so full of himself sometimes I just want to laugh. I am smiling now as I write it, because his pomposity—"suburban sensibilities" indeed!—is just too much. Yet, he can pull it off better than any other man I've known, that's for certain.

And he was right. Punishment it was, though with delicious and certainly unexpected results! I opted for touching myself, of course. The thought of putting my mouth on a man's thing! No way! I do feel like a liberated lover, since I've been with Mr. Stevenson, but that is not something I could ever do!

Now, I have touched myself before, but it's never amounted to much. It seems kind of silly really, and I've never been in the right situation, I guess. The rare times I've tried—Frank's last overnight hunting trip comes to mind—I usually just stop, feeling stupid, unable to concentrate on whatever sexy image I've tried to conjure in my head.

But that day was different. Just like each day with Mr. Stevenson. When I really give myself over to him, the most amazing things seem to happen and that day was no exception.

First, I just stood there staring at him. He stared back, his gaze penetrating me, making me shift and shuffle in front of him. "Well, slave?"

"I really couldn't—" I hedged, but he interrupted me, telling me I didn't have that choice. Which was it to be? I stood there a while longer, gaping like an idiot.

He said, "Actually, that's not entirely true. You do have a choice. You always have a choice, in fact. That choice is to pack up and go, or stay and do as you're told. And my offer still stands. I will give you excellent references and two weeks pay, in addition to whatever is owed to you."

The guy should play poker. Maybe he does. I sure can't. I realized with absolute certainty as he held out this ultimatum that I didn't want to do that. As embarrassing as it would be to touch myself in front of this man, I didn't want to go. To never experience this heightened sensuality that permeates my life now! To never feel that thrill again! And so I bowed my head and said, "I'll touch myself, Master."

"Speak up, I can't hear you when you mumble, slave."

I cleared my throat, feeling the burn in my face and said louder, "I'll touch myself, Master." He smiled, his lips tilting upwards just a hint as he pointed me to his couch.

"Very good, slave. I'm delighted you have the courage to proceed. You have great promise. Beyond my expectations, I assure you."

Whatever that meant. Anyway, he directed me to the couch and told me not to strip, which was a relief. He just wanted the blouse to remain open and for me to hike up my skirt and remove my panties. I have to say I felt like a real slut sitting like that.

I was so embarrassed I couldn't meet his eyes. I started rubbing around on myself, feeling terribly anxious. After a few minutes he said, "Slow down. Take your time. I can see this isn't something you're used to doing. I'm going to guide you. Close your eyes."

I did and he told me to spread my legs farther, and lean back more comfortably against the sofa. Then he told me to lick my fingers and bring them down to my pussy.

His word. "That's it," he said, his voice soothing. "You look so beautiful like that, Olivia. So sexy. So perfect." Well, I did like hearing that and I guess it calmed me a little. Because I felt ridiculous exposed like that in front of him! But he really sounded sincere when he said he found my bared sex beautiful.

I tried again, trying for the light fluttery feeling he had invoked in me the few times he's touched me like that. It started to feel good, and I sighed with pleasure and leaned back. I was keenly aware of his eyes on me. On my bared breasts, on my naked thighs and, of course, my sex, though at least it was obscured now by my fingers.

"Yes," I heard him murmur, "Yes." It felt good. I think knowing he was watching me, while embarrassing, even humiliating, was also what made it so exciting. So different from my own occasional fumblings.

It was his words, though, that really got to me. Because he started to talk to me, saying things that would have offended me in any other context, but which made my blood fairly boil with lust.

"Olivia. You are my slut. You bare yourself for me and make yourself come for me because you belong to me. Right now, I could call in someone, say Mr. Hawkins, and I could say to him, this is Olivia. My slave. She does what I tell her. She's a slut. And you know what you would do? You would stay right where you are and keep rubbing yourself like the slut you are, until I told you to stop."

Thank God, he didn't demand a response, because what he was saying was outrageous, if I'd processed it with my brain. But my brain was shut down, or subverted, or something, and his words went straight down, mixing with my fingers, making me dizzy, wanton, crazy. Then something started to happen. Something that's never happened to me before, and I realize now what it was.

I had an orgasm.

Not just a little shudder or tingle, like I've had before, when champagne has been involved, and desire has pushed me along. No. This was different. There was no question. No, "was it or wasn't it?" like I've wondered before. I climaxed, and hard. And while it was happening, I wasn't embarrassed, or shy, or even aware of Mr. Stevenson for that brief suspended moment in time. I was just sensation. Pure raw sensual ecstasy.

And I did it myself! I must have left the planet for a moment or two, because when I came back to myself Mr. Stevenson was kneeling right in front of me, his hands on either of my bare thighs.

"You never cease to surprise me, Olivia," he said, smiling broadly. Gently he brought my thighs together, and smoothed my hair from my forehead. It was a lover's touch.

I felt completely spent. It was like I had run a race. I also felt wonderful—euphoric. That's the word. In a flash, I suddenly understood what all the "hoopla" was about. This is what the men were after! Hell, why wouldn't they be! This is better than ice cream!

chapter 8

Tess couldn't help but laugh out. Nana was still Nana, after all. Utterly charming and a little silly. Imagine not experiencing a real orgasm until you were twenty-nine years old and had already given birth to three children!

Brad's spin on the entry was a little different. "Would you do that for me, Tess?" he said, his tone playful but his expression intense. "Would you spread your legs for me, at the office, and make yourself come?"

Tess laughed lightly. "Oh, yeah, right. At the office. Which one of us would be accused of sexual harassment when they caught us, huh?"

"Who says we'd be caught? I rather like the idea. I want you to come for me, Tess. At the illustrious offices of Reilly & Clark."

_*_

It was six o'clock and while most of the support staff were gone or packing up, many of the attorneys were still hard at work, or milling about in the open areas of the large suite of offices, discussing cases or just shooting the breeze.

In Brad's office sat Tess, fully clothed in her cream-colored suit and soft silk blouse. But the blouse was unbuttoned, revealing high, young breasts, the dark pink nipples still hidden in folds of silk. Her skirt was hiked up, revealing the lacy tops of sheer thigh-high stockings. Brad sat behind his desk, which was, as usual, covered in papers and files in seemingly haphazard fashion.

If his secretary had stuck her head in, she might not have noticed Tess, sitting on the long leather couch on the far side of the office, out of the line of vision of the door. But if she had entered the room she would have seen the half-naked slut, legs apart, fingers buried in her pussy.

When they'd first worked together on a case, Brad had found Tess attractive, sure. What wasn't to like about her dark, glossy hair, her large hazel eyes, that small, but lush mouth, just made for kissing? He'd admired her lithe figure, as far as he could see it in the proper linen suits she wore for work, with skirts that fell just below the knee and sensible pumps on small, delicate feet.

While he'd fantasized a time or two about throwing her down amidst the myriad of papers and files on the long, smooth boardroom table, he'd never dreamed back then this girl, this ravishing, sensual woman, would one day belong to him.

That he could command her to pull open her clothing and, right in the his office, rub her wet, hot cunt like the slut she was beneath the proper demeanor. Brad reached into his suit trousers, unbending his rising cock and giving it a few stiff strokes.

He could see the flush on her cheeks and throat and the giveaway tremble of her body that Tess was nearing climax. Now for the test. "Stop," Brad ordered.

Unlike the time at the restaurant, this time she obeyed him, opening her eyes in question, shifting to cover herself, her eyes glancing nervously toward his office door.

"No one's coming." Brad answered her unspoken question. "I just don't want you to come yet. Not yet. You'll wait for permission." Tess took a deep, shuddery breath. He knew she wanted to come and had been so close. He also know she craved what he offered. She wanted to relinquish control of her orgasms. Brad would decide when she came, or if she came. The idea moved both of them in a primal way that went beyond words.

Brad watched the internal struggle and then a certain calm settle over Tess's features. Brushing the hair from her eyes, she sat up straighter and started to pull down her skirt. "No," Brad said. "Leave it that way, hiked up like a common whore. Come over here and get on your knees. Right here." He was pointing under his large maple wood desk, as he pushed back from it on the wheels of his large leather chair.

Tess stared at him, realization dawning in her eyes. She hoisted herself from the leather couch and began to walk toward him. "No. Crawl." He waited a beat, wondering if he'd gone too far. Would she refuse?

Staring at him with wide eyes, Tess dropped slowly to the carpet and crawled toward her lover, her skirt hiked over her ass, her panties a silky puddle left behind. She knelt, disheveled, her blouse hanging open, at Brad's feet.

He unbuckled his belt, opened his pants and pulled away his shirt, revealing his large cock, straining and erect in his underwear.

With sure fingers, Tess slid the cotton fabric down, releasing the erect member. She flashed an impish, decidedly un-submissive grin toward Brad, who despite himself grinned back. This really wasn't the smartest thing he ever did, having a colleague suck him off at the office, but he was no longer thinking with his big head, that was for sure.

Tess bent over him, gliding her tongue up and down Brad's shaft for several moments, making him, if possible, even harder than before. With cool hands cupping his balls and the base of his shaft, she lowered her head down and down, taking his entire cock back into her throat, staying perfectly still.

The pleasure was nearly unbearable and he knew he was seconds away from orgasm. She slowly pulled back, using her throat muscles to tighten and ease the pressure as she gently squeezed his aching balls. At that moment it was Tess who was in complete control.

Though it felt fantastic, Brad decided to bring the focus back to Tess. He pushed at her head, forcing her to release her heavenly clutch on his cock. She looked up at him in surprise. "What's the matter?"

"It's wonderful, Tess. You give the best head on the planet. But I want something more from you right now. I want this to be a truly submissive act. Right now, you're calling the shots. I want to take that from you. To put you in a more submissive head space."

He paused a moment, working out a plan. "I have an idea. Get up." Brad stood and held out his hand, his cock still bobbing lewdly from his open pants.

He led her to the private bathroom just off his office. Removing his tie, he directed Tess to kneel on the little bath rug. He tied her wrists together behind her back with his tie and then pulled her blouse completely open.

"You look so hot, slut. So hot. Are you wet for me?" He reached down, grabbing her cunt, pressing two fingers into her wet slit, making her moan. He could feel the muscles inside contracting against his fingers, which were slick with her desire.

Feeling power and lust mingle and blend into one erotic force, Brad licked his lips as he stared down at his beautiful sub girl. "You're too good at sucking cock, baby. We have to make it harder for you. No hands, and you aren't on top now. You're going to kneel there and I'm going to fuck your face, got it? You're going to swallow it all when I come. Or I might come on your face and breasts. I'll have to see what I feel like doing when the time comes."

Tess nodded, her large eyes fixed on his face and then flickering down to his cock, giving it a decidedly hungry look. Brad laughed with pleasure as he leaned over her, guiding his sizable cock into her mouth.

Tess closed her eyes, letting the penis slide past her lips and into her throat. Brad knew this angle made it more difficult to relax her throat. She gagged slightly as he began to thrust in and out. "Open yourself for me, Tess. Don't resist me. You don't control the rhythm, I do. Now take it."

He grabbed either side of her head and guided himself down into her throat, holding her still as he began to thrust in and out of her mouth. She couldn't swallow and a trail of drool spilled down her chin, but with hands tied and his cock stuffed down her throat she couldn't do anything about it.

He was careful, though, always pulling back before it got dangerous, allowing her to draw her breath before he plunged back, taking her mouth and throat with his sexual weapon. He could almost feel the panic mingled with desire, creating a potent and heady mixture of lust and fear inside Tess. He felt connected to her, as if he were not only the one doing this to her, but it was being done to him as well.

Aware he was about to come, Brad pulled away, pushing Tess down and onto her side. With her hands still secured above her ass, he crouched on his side behind her and thrust his cock into her wet and needy cunt, filling her up so that she screamed with pleasure, forgetting where she was and who might overhear them. Brad clamped his hand over her mouth, hissing in her ear to be quiet, as he rutted with fierce passion into her.

He came hard, his hand still clamped over Tess's mouth. Finally he let her go, pulling out of her clinging heat to roll onto his back.

"Brad," Tess whined. "What about me? I didn't come!"

Brad felt an evil smile slide over his lips. "You want to come, huh, slut? Isn't it enough to satisfy your Master? Olivia never would have begged to come." His voice was teasing but still he left her bound and needy on the floor as he stood up.

"Please," she moaned.

"Beg for it."

"Please. Do it, Brad. Make me come. Please, please, please. I need you."

She looked so beautiful lying there, arms pinned behind her back, legs akimbo, her bare sex red and swollen. Carefully he rolled his lover onto her back, leaving her arms bound behind her. Pushing her skirt out of the way, Brad spread Tess's legs and leaned down to her sticky-sweet cunt.

Slowly he slid his tongue along the swollen labia, drawing a sweet sigh from the girl. She arched up, pulling at her restraints, her voice a mewling pant of lust. Brad increased the tempo of his kisses, drawing low, feral moans from his lover. Her body began to buck and tremble and he held on, riding the waves of her passion. Still he held her until the little after-tremors of pleasure that shook her were stilled.

Nuzzling her ear, he whispered, "Was it better than ice cream?"

~*~

December 12, 1961

I'm having a harder time keeping things separate. I find myself daydreaming about him while making a sandwich for Sandra, or helping Jeannie with her homework. Ever since the day he made me touch myself for him—ever since I found that sweet sensation, something has changed for me.

And yet, I know I mustn't let it. I don't think it's that I'm in love with him. I'm not. And I still love Frank, of course I do. I think it's just moved to another level. I find myself doing things to try to get him to respond. He seems to be gentler somehow, sweeter. The odd thing is I don't want that. I don't want the "sweet" Mr. Stevenson. I like the stern taskmaster. I know that's bizarre, but there you are.

The man with the ruler, tap, tap, tapping on the edge of my chair and then smacking my bottom while I squirm and feel the heat of the sting melt into a fiery desire inside of me. That's still there, but something has altered somehow. Is the elusive Mr. Stevenson "getting involved"? Worse still, am I?

I forced the issue. I guess I'm not very "submissive". Mr. Stevenson seemed almost amused when I approached him and I must have blushed twelve shades of red. You could have cooked eggs on my face!

I can admit it here, since it's only me reading these secret words, but I did try to manipulate the situation. And I guess I succeeded. Or maybe he did—I'm not even sure at this point. I just know I was missing our little "punishment sessions". Ever since I orgasmed in front of him, he's been treating me a little differently. Like I mentioned before—more like a lover, less like the naughty schoolgirl. It's funny to write that, since at first that got me so mad, but now, I admit, it sets me on fire.

I guess I was pouting. His word. "Don't pout, Olivia, it isn't becoming." I guess I had been moping around for a few days. No ruler. No sexy sting that goes zipping right to my sex when he "punishes" me. I actually tried using the ruler myself when he was at lunch but it was just silly. Didn't do a thing for me. I guess it's all of it together—the fact that Mr. Stevenson is the one doing it and that I've been a "naughty girl". I feel so alive when it's happening!

I've even tried some of those old ploys, messing up on purpose, sloshing his coffee, forgetting a file, leaving a sentence out of a letter.

The one thing I didn't do, didn't dare to do, was come out and ask for it. Admit aloud to him that I was craving the sweet heat of a spanking. Remembering the hot licking kiss of his whip against my flesh. Oh, my God. I'm reading this now—what I just wrote. I want to be whipped! Surely, this is wicked and evil?

And yet, I don't believe it is. Just because I've been taught to behave and feel a certain way—that doesn't make it the only way, does it? Mr. Stevenson has explained it, and whenever he talks about it, it makes perfect sense. Submission, he says, freely given and lovingly taken is the ultimate sensual expression. What evil or harm can there be in a consensual exchange of power? And when he says it, it makes sense.

It's only when I'm alone, riding on the bus home, thinking of dull, but dear Frank who would never begin to comprehend what I'm experiencing, and would be too horrified to even try and understand. That's when I worry I am a sick ticket.

While I feel a great excitement and vitality as I discover this bizarre but thrilling lifestyle, I feel I am betraying Frank on yet another level, because I'm leaving him behind emotionally. I'm not trying to share or understand what is happening to me with him. But how could I? Even if I had these feelings of submission and masochism without another man being involved—even if it were only in theory and something in my head, Frank would never understand. Not in a million years.

Not that I blame him. He has no frame of reference except our little safe world, where everything is always as it seems, and sex is for procreation or to satisfy the man's "baser" needs and has nothing to do with the thrill of danger, or stolen joys.

And so, using that as rationalization I suppose, I go on, getting deeper and deeper into whatever it is Mr. Stevenson and I have. But I digress, as usual.

After the little attempts to force a session from him, Mr. Stevenson did finally call me into his office, using the one word intonation of my name that usually portends something dangerous and sexy. I entered, trying to look calm, already feeling my panties moisten with expectation.

But instead of ordering me to drape myself over the couch or lift my skirt and stand in the corner, he said, "We need to talk. Please sit down."

I was surprised but obeyed, feeling a little let down, but curious. He explained, "Olivia. I know what you're doing. And I even understand why you're doing it. You have come to crave the very 'punishments' that are designed to prevent you from making the careless mistakes that you are now making on purpose. Am I correct?" I started to deny it, even though it was true, but he cut me off.

"Please. If you are going to lie and pretend not to understand, save us both time and go back to your desk. I want you to be honest, my dear. And to tell you the truth, I am not displeased that you have come to long for the pain and erotic humiliation that you now appreciate can deeply intensify any interaction. You are coming along, in fact, as a true submissive and I'm delighted.

"That's why I think it's time we dispense with these little games, because that's really what they are. You are an excellent secretary and I hate to think you're making errors just to satisfy your little lusts. In spite of our unique relationship, we do in fact have a law office to run." He actually grinned at me as I ducked my head, feeling like a fool. The man understands me sometimes better than I do myself! I was all ears though I was now staring at my shoes.

"Olivia. I think you're ready for more. What we shared that night at the hotel was unique. I think I've pulled back some because I was afraid of the intensity of our feelings. We are, though we don't often discuss it, both married and we have our families to consider. The very nature of a relationship like ours can be so intense that sometimes one can confuse the sensual desire and need to submit or dominate with actual love.

"No, that isn't what I mean to say precisely. It is a kind of love, but it isn't something you and I can afford to actualize in any deeper sense. Any permanent sense—" He seemed to be floundering and I looked up to see that he, the impervious Mr. Stevenson, was actually blushing. Well, not all-out red as a beet, like I get, but definitely a darker shade of pink than is natural for him.

I knew what he meant, and he looked so uncomfortable that I took pity on the poor man and said, "You mean, you don't want me to get the wrong idea and think we're having a love affair that's going to lead to us ditching our spouses and running off together. Right? Well, don't you worry, Mr. Stevenson. I'm on the same page as you there! I've got three kids who need their daddy and despite what we have here, whatever that is, I do love the guy!"

He looked relieved and smiled. "Then we do understand one another," he said, back in control. "Which is excellent, as the new phase of your training may make you peculiarly vulnerable and I would never want to take advantage of that."

I'm not quite sure what he meant, but I sure understood the next part! "So, what I want to do is dispense with the punishment rules. I will still punish you if I feel it necessary, but now you are ready for something else. I am going to teach you about the pleasure of pain."

The pleasure of pain.

The words still echo in my head. When he said them I felt the usual confusion of my brain saying that was crazy and made no sense, but my body quietly smiled, opening itself to his words, understanding the secret language as if I were born speaking it.

I can barely sit now as I write this. I'm definitely marked. At first, I was angry and frightened! What if Frank saw the bruises? Delicate little marks cover my buttocks from that spanking. But I'll just have to be careful, I suppose. It's not a sex night anyway in Frank's little schedule and I should easily be able to avoid detection.

And I did learn more about the pleasure of pain. Looking back, I can see that the lessons have been building slowly over these months. Little increments. The whipping at the hotel was pretty intense, but I realize now he held back. I think the *idea* of the whip was as powerful as anything. He was actually quite gentle, in retrospect.

That spanking yesterday was something else again. While it was happening, at least at first, I didn't quite appreciate the "pleasure" aspect of the pain! It just plain hurt! Mr. Stevenson had me lay across his lap on his couch. He of course was fully clothed, and he didn't have me strip completely. In a way, what he did was more embarrassing. He made me remove my panties and lift my skirt to my waist.

His eyes raked my bare body as I was forced to hold up my skirt for his appraisal. I can't describe the potent mixture of humiliation and excitement that is engendered in me when he does that! When he just stares at me like I'm an object. A sex object. To be used or not, as he decrees.

This time he said, "You're going to get a real spanking today, slave. I'm going to spank you until I'm ready to stop. You can cry out, as you wish. But I don't want you to try and get away and I don't want you to tell me to stop. I'll stop when I'm ready. This will be your first test in this new phase of submission. It will hurt at first, but if I know you, and I do, you will find that the artificial line we draw between pain and pleasure will blur and you will experience the true ecstasy of pure sensation."

Wow! I wish I could talk like he does. Poetry. Luckily, I can remember it long enough to write it down. And, though I was nervous and not really focused on what he was saying at the time, I think I'm starting to understand.

I lay across his scratchy suit pants, feeling the hard bulge of his erection, which pleased me. He can keep his voice as cold as steel, but his body betrays him to be just as warm-blooded as the next fellow.

Lying across his lap, I wriggled, trying to get comfortable, finding myself suddenly having trouble catching my breath. His hands were smooth and cool against my bottom at first, stroking me gently as if he were preparing the flesh for what was to come.

Then a smack, light at first. I was reminded of the whipping and of how long he had taken to slowly increase the tempo and intensity of the lashing. This time wasn't so gradual however, as after just a few light smacks with his open palm he really let go. The sound of flesh on flesh resounded in the room, though it was a fraction of a second before I registered the stinging pain of the strike. Believe it or not, it hurt more than the whipping!

And after twenty or thirty of those hard-handed spankings, it hurt way more! At first I tried to be dignified—as dignified as you can be, lying with your skirt up around your waist, buck-naked on the knees of a fully clothed man!—and I only moaned a little and tried to stay still.

I could feel my skin starting to heat up and each stinging slap only made it worse. After just a few minutes, I forgot about trying to be quiet or still, and I was wailing and wiggling like a crazy thing! One time, I put my hands back, trying to protect my poor sore bottom and he smacked them just as hard until I pulled them away!

I wasn't thinking any of those lofty thoughts of his about pain transmuting to pleasure or the sublime ecstasy of submission. I was thinking how I could shift to avoid that hard palm! It hurt! I started to beg and tell him I couldn't do it and to let me up right then! But he wouldn't listen!

Instead he kept smacking me, as he quietly said, "Take it, slave. It's what you need. It's what you were born for." Here's the strangest thing. When I heard that, somehow I calmed down. The panic that had been rising in my throat seemed to recede and I was aware suddenly of the heat in my sex. Of the desire rising alongside the sting on my flesh.

He kept on smacking me and while it did still hurt, something was different. Maybe it was just the perception, but then, isn't perception everything?

All I know is, the pain was no longer something to be avoided. It had indeed transmuted somehow. Not to pleasure precisely but to something more than that. Some kind of alloy that was stronger than either pleasure or pain alone. This was what he was talking about—I knew it on a gut level, though at the time all I knew, or experienced, was that I wanted what he was doing.

Craved it.

Longed for it.

Needed it.

I stilled on his lap and he continued to slap and smack my bottom, still saying those sexy hypnotic words about submission and desire. Then his hand slipped down to my sex and I spread my legs like a slut, unable to stifle the moan he wrested from me with his fingers.

I can't describe it. Words fail. I just know I wanted it. I didn't want it to stop. His use of the word "slave" is more apt than he knows. And as usual, as I write this in retrospect, barely capturing the emotion, I realize I am afraid.

Where is this going? How long can it go on?

chapter 9

THEY'D ALWAYS SPENT their nights together at Tess's place, since Brad had a roommate. But tonight the roommate, Peter, was out of town on business and Brad had invited Tess to come to his place.

"I have a surprise for you," he'd explained, a glint in his eye.

Brad's place was nice, nicer than Tess had expected. She realized she'd been imagining the typical "bachelor pad" complete with empty pizza boxes, beer cans, magazines, dirty dishes and bookshelves built from planks and crates.

Instead, Brad owned a spacious three-bedroom house in a much nicer part of town than Tess could afford. His roommate leased space from him, to help cover the mortgage. The high-ceilinged living room was tastefully furnished with soft red leather couches and chairs, blond hardwood floors, with handspun rugs placed here and there, and large attractive abstracts on the walls.

"This is really nice," she said and Brad laughed, noting that she sounded surprised. He led her to the kitchen, a modern affair with granite counters and a stainless steel gas range and refrigerator.

"Impressive," she said, looking around. "Someone around here is a cook!"

"That would be Peter, actually," Brad said. "Though I can make a mean chicken parmesan." He opened a bottle of chardonnay and poured a glass for Tess.

Tess took a long drink of the cold, crisp wine and said, "Did someone mention a surprise?" She loved surprises of any kind but had a feeling this one wasn't a vase of flowers or a new book. She was right.

Brad led her into a room that held exercise equipment, including a treadmill, a weight-lifting machine and the requisite free weights piled in a corner. But what made her catch her breath was what was hanging from the ceiling. Two large hooks had been screwed into the ceiling and dangling from them were thick metal chains, at the end of which were black leather cuffs, each held closed with a thick metal clip. On the ground beneath them was a two-foot pole of metal, with a cuff attached at either end.

"What in the world?" Tess didn't finish the sentence but she knew even before she asked what this was. This was her dream. The fantasy. The one where she was tethered in a room, stretched and helpless, while the man in shadows held the whip, as yet unused...

Brad nodded at her and said softly, "I'm going to whip you, just like the man in your dreams." She saw the whip then. A large flogger of black leather with complicated knots at the base of a long, thick handle.

"Where did you get that?" she breathed, awestruck.

"Online, of course. You can get anything online, you know that." As he spoke, Brad unbuttoned the top button of Tess's jeans, and pulled at the zipper. He pulled them past her slim hips, taking the silky panties down with them.

"I like you with your pants around your feet," he sang lightly, paraphrasing the lyrics from a popular song. Taking her arms, he said, "Don't move," while he lifted her T-shirt, revealing her low-cut pink satin bra. Reaching around her, he unclasped the bra, releasing her breasts.

Through it all, Tess just stood there, her eyes shining, her heart thumping. Her cheeks felt hot and it felt somehow as if reality were heightened. Colors were brighter, sound was magnified, movements were slowed.

She stood completely naked, her chest softly rising and falling. Brad moved closer, leaning down to gently pull Tess's hair back from her face. He kissed her neck, his lips closing over the little pulse that betrayed her excitement.

Kneeling at her feet, he gently took one ankle and closed a leather cuff around it, buckling it snugly in place. Spreading her legs, he locked the second ankle in place, forcing Tess to stand with her legs spread, unable now to close them.

He stood, raising Tess's right arm, taking the wrist and clipping it into the leather cuff that dangled from its chain. Once he'd secured the left arm, Tess was indeed stretched taut and helpless, naked and defenseless before her lover.

She was breathing hard, though Brad still hadn't touched her with the flogger. He lifted it, drawing it through his hands in front of her, showing her its long, thick leather strips, shiny and black, knotted securely at the handle. He held the flogger close to her face and said quietly, "Kiss it."

Tess's eyes widened, and for a moment, she stared at Brad, barely recognizing her boyfriend who stared at her now with a stern, almost forbidding expression, his eyes hooded with lust. Her breath still caught in her throat and she jerked at her restraints, something near panic rising in her gut.

Brad lowered the whip and leaned down, gently kissing her lips. "Tess. It's me. It's only me. But I want this to be real. Not a game. I want you to show your subservience and your desire to suffer for me with this symbolic act. Kiss the whip, Tess."

He lifted it again, bringing it close to Tess's face. Tess wanted it real too. If only she could stop her heart from slamming so hard in her chest. She took a deep breath and let it out slowly before touching the cold leather with a chaste press of her lips.

This time Brad's kiss wasn't so gentle and nor was Tess's ardent response. As nervous as she was, she was also on fire with lust, her pussy wet and throbbing between her legs. She kissed him feverishly, willing him to stay, since she couldn't hold him close with arms that were bound high above her. He pulled away, his cock straining in his jeans.

Brad stepped behind Tess. She turned her head to follow his actions. "Eyes straight ahead," he commanded and she turned her face forward, biting her lip in anticipation, her ass tingling.

When she felt the glide of leather slide over her ass, she jumped and gasped but she didn't say stop. He did it again, this time a little harder, a little surer. Tess remained still as he began to smack her ass in a steady beat of leather against flesh. It stung, yes, but it also felt good, or, more accurately, it felt right.

But when the stinging leather moved its way up Tess's back, she yelped and jerked. "Ow," she cried out, as the flogger heated and stung her flesh. Her heart was pounding so hard she could hear it in her ears, and she was breathing so fast she thought she would fall down if she hadn't been held in leather and chains. The flogger moved back down to her ass, striking with some force now, forcing her forward with each blow.

God, it was happening. The fantasy was becoming reality, but Tess wasn't processing it with her mind. She was raw feeling, hot needy passion, aching sexual desire. She loved the fiery sting of the lash—it was as if her body had been waiting for this all her life, though she hadn't known it completely until this second.

"Fuck me!" she screamed, suddenly desperate for his cock, his warmth, his kisses. Yet he continued, his breathing labored behind her as he brought the black leather strips down upon her trembling flesh again and again.

"No," she began, barely aware she was speaking. "No, no, no, no..." It wasn't precisely a plea, but more of an incantation, which shifted as he continued the flogging to, "Yes, yes, yes, yes..."

Finally, pushed to the very edge of what she could tolerate, Tess begged in a hoarse, ragged voice, "Please. Please fuck me!"

At last Brad dropped the flogger. Stripping off his T-shirt, he pressed his body against her heated flesh and brought his arms around her from behind, cupping her breasts in his hands.

"God, you are so perfect," he breathed in her ear, kissing her neck, grinding his pelvis against her hot ass. They were, she realized, both sweating, their skin slick and warm.

He unclipped her ankles and released her wrists. Catching her as she fell back, he lifted the spent girl into his arms and carried her to his bedroom, dropping her on the black silk coverlet. She watched him, barely able to focus as he kicked off his jeans. He stared at her with a lust so raw it nearly frightened her.

Falling over her, he plunged into her wetness, barely giving her body a chance to adjust to his girth. She jerked and moaned beneath him, bringing her arms and legs around him to pull him deeper.

"You're mine!" he whispered fiercely. He took her hard and rough, taking what was his.

Tess clung to him, drawing him deeper into her, holding him fast. He arched and bucked, moaning his pleasure. "And you're mine," she whispered back, never more certain of something in her life.

_*_

December 19, 1961
Mr. Stevenson says I am very obedient but that it's easy to be obedient when you want just what is happening to you. I do obey him but he's right, as usual. I want to do it. I thrill to his command. "Olivia," he says, in that reso-

nant voice and it's as if something flips on inside of me, and I become his slave girl. Obedient and aroused, ready to do his bidding.

I know it's a game. I mean, it can never be more than that, but sometimes it feels more real than anything else in my life. It's as if my life at home is just marking time until I can return to the office and become Mr. Stevenson's slave.

Sometimes when I'm just doing something mundane—setting the table or playing with the children, or doing needlepoint while Frank sits beside me watching the game—suddenly I wonder if they can tell. If I look different somehow. If I've been "marked" in some secret way by Mr. Stevenson and the life I live in secret away from home.

Mostly I can put it aside at home. I have to. I am a mother first, of course, and I have a duty to my family. But when Livvie leaves home on Monday morning, and gets on that bus, something happens. I can almost feel it, as if it were a physical thing. Ditzy Livvie becomes calm and graceful Olivia.

Once I put on my sexy panties and garters and apply that bright red lipstick Mr. Stevenson favors, the transformation is complete. When he arrives, I bring him his coffee and wait by his desk for his orders for the day. Most of them concern the running of the office, but usually something sexy is thrown in. But as he has observed, it's something I want to do.

Like when he has me bend over his desk so he can inspect some part of me. That makes me blush like crazy but at the same time, it excites me to the point that I actually tremble! The other day he had me lie back against his desk. He pushed my dress up and put his hand in my panties. His fingers were like fire probing against me, turning me to jelly with desire.

I am such a slut now! Frank would die. But I love what Mr. Stevenson does with his hand. I can't do it to myself. Not like he does. And he's so casual about it. He likes to watch me squirm and moan. The other day his hands were in my panties and I was so close—oh, so deliciously close to climax when the phone rang!

I found myself hoping he would just let it ring but Mr. Stevenson was expecting an important call and he picked up the receiver! Normally, I screen all the calls for him but now he said, "James Stevenson," calmly into the phone, all business, his hand still buried in my panties.

I was embarrassed to say the least! The spell was broken and instead of feeling sexy and exotic, I felt ridiculous lying among his papers with my legs splayed and dress hiked up. I started to sit up but he pushed me back down and mouthed the words, "Stay there."

"Ah, good morning, George. No, not at all. Oh, yes, she's, uh, busy, at the moment so I took the call myself. Now about our meeting, you'll be able to make it?" He listened for a while, his fingers still teasing me, drawing the need out of me and then he said, "Excellent. Olivia and I will be ready for you. I think you'll be quite pleased. Good, good. See you at 11:00. Goodbye."

Olivia? Was he talking about me? I presumed he was talking to George Hawkins, an important client and also a friend. They sometimes had lunch together and had gone to college together. What was I going to be ready for? Usually when a client was coming for a meeting, I was informed in advance if I was to attend to take notes, or to fill them in on certain aspects of a brief I was working on.

Mr. Stevenson pressed my thighs apart and thrust a finger up inside of me. I moaned and shifted, though I was still distracted by the phone call. I forgot all about it, though, when his fingers did their magic dance on me. Then dimly I heard him say, "Remember I told you that you were obedient because it was easy for you? Today I'm going to test your obedience in a more dramatic way. Do you wish to obey me, slave?"

I nodded, suddenly unsure but wanting to appear as if I were. Anything to keep his fingers on my sex. A few more of those perfect strokes and I was done for. I moaned and pressed into his hands like a harlot, shivering and shuddering with pleasure.

I lay there for a while, still sprawled against his desk and trying to recover my composure. Mr. Stevenson said, "George Hawkins is aware of our, uh, unique arrangement."

That got my attention.

"Excuse me?" I sat up, flustered, scattering his papers as I did so. I wobbled on my heels and made it over to his couch, knowing I must look a mess, still feeling the delicious heat in my blood from the orgasm. But along with the heat was a sick, cold feeling as I processed his words.

"He knows? About us? I mean, this?" I waved vaguely around the room but he knew what I meant and he nodded. George Hawkins had often been in our offices and had never been anything but polite, though he was always very friendly and easygoing. He doesn't stand on the formality that means so much to Mr. Stevenson.

"Yes. George is very progressive. He understands about this kind of thing. Even shares our, uh, predilections. We both discovered certain, uh, literature, in college, that confirmed for each of us our dominant impulses. He's never had the luxury of experiencing it firsthand.

"I took the liberty of sharing with him about what you and I have together. I took the chance that you would understand. That you were far enough along in your training to be obedient in the face of a witness. Do you think you can do that, Olivia? Submit in front of another man?"

"No." I just blurted that out.

No way.

That was my first impulse. It was one thing to play this game with Mr. Stevenson. We had an understanding! But another man! What in God's name was he thinking?

"You answer too quickly," he said. His mouth was a thin line and I could see the disapproval, the disappointment, on his face. I didn't want to disappoint him but how could he ask that of me?

As if reading my mind he offered, "I'm not asking that you submit in any sexual way to Mr. Hawkins. I understand your reservations in that regard. No, it would be a simple show of submission. I will probably ask you to display yourself. To show him your grace during punishment. No more than that. Surely, you could do that for me, slave. Just that?"

I bit my lip, thinking about it. One part of me said no, absolutely not, no way, never. Another part of me felt kind of melty. That's not the right word, but that's what it felt like. A sort of melty, edgy feeling. I realized with a little shock that I actually wanted to do it. That it would be terribly exciting and daring to show another person, another man, what I did with Mr. Stevenson!

I've never been able to share it with another living soul! How could I? And who would possibly understand? And yet, Mr. Stevenson had assured me so many times that I took punishment with grace and that he was pleased with that. And that he finds my body lovely and sexy. No man has ever paid the attention he pays to my body. I feel so taken care of around him. Even when he hurts me—especially when he hurts me, I feel consumed by him—completely and properly adored.

Slowly I nodded. I was afraid, but excited. Mr. Stevenson nodded back, clearly pleased. "I'm proud of you, Olivia. You thought it through and didn't just react to your gut. Sometimes I wonder what would have happened if we'd met at another time..." He didn't finish the sentence, but he didn't have to. It was idle speculation and obviously would lead nowhere so I put it out of my head, as I'm sure he did, and I went back to my desk.

While they may have shared certain "predilections" Mr. Hawkins obviously didn't share Mr. Stevenson's passion for punctuality. Eleven o'clock came and went as I remained at my desk, nervous as a mouse in a cat's bed. I didn't even pretend to type, but just kept organizing my blotter, moving things here and there, fidgeting and glancing at the clock which is hung just across from my desk on the opposite wall.

Finally, at 11:22 a.m. there came the familiar jingle as someone opened the outer door to our building. The office door opened and in came George Hawkins, a short, slim man, also in his mid-thirties, though if I didn't know that, I would have thought he was barely out of college. His face is round and pink and he hardly looks as if he needs to shave.

His voice was surprisingly deep for such a slight man, as he greeted me with a grin. "Good morning, Olivia. Nice to see you again." Perfectly proper but I blushed nonetheless, now that I knew he knew about us. He hung his hat on a peg as Mr. Stevenson came out to greet him.

"George. Glad you could make it—at last." Mr. Stevenson looked pointedly at his watch. George just laughed.

"Olivia," Mr. Stevenson said, coming fully into the room. "You remember George Hawkins."

I nodded, feeling foolish. Of course I remembered him! I murmured, "Good morning, Mr. Hawkins."

"Please," he grinned. "Call me George! This is the sixties, for God's sake! Not the nineteenth century. Your Mr. Stevenson might stand on formalities but not me! I'm a modern man." He laughed, making fun of himself and at the same time putting me much more at ease. I liked him.

But that didn't mean I was ready for what was to come. Mr. Stevenson invited George into his office. I brought in the coffee, putting it in the nice silver coffee service Mr. Stevenson keeps for special occasions.

I poured for them, declining when George asked if I'd join them in a cup. The last thing I needed was caffeine! I was so jittery already, I felt like a windup doll. After I served them, I wasn't sure if I was supposed to stay or go. They were chattering away about some old college tales as if I wasn't even in the room.

I decided to leave and come back when they called for me.

If they called for me.

I turned to go and was stopped by Mr. Stevenson's voice. "Olivia. Don't leave. We have need of you."

An odd way to put it. I turned around, half expecting him to ask me to take dictation—that's how formal he sounded. I realized suddenly that perhaps he was as uncomfortable as I was or at least as nervous. No, not as nervous, surely, but somewhat on edge perhaps. Well, it was his game, so let him be the one to worry!

I smiled, trying to look demure and sexy at the same time. I don't think it worked. I felt foolish and shy, so I just looked down, waiting, trying not to fidget.

"Olivia. As you know, Mr. Hawkins here is interested in a little, uh, demonstration. He's aware of your submissive nature and is looking forward to a display of your obedience."

I found that I wasn't breathing. I tried to take some air, to clear my head, but I could only gasp a little. I kept looking at my shoes, wondering if the floor would take pity on me and open up to swallow me whole. It didn't.

Instead, Mr. Stevenson said, "Olivia. Show Mr. Hawkins your pretty garters." I didn't move for a moment. I just stood there thinking *so now it begins*. He was asking me to lift my skirt for this stranger. But it was more than that, of course. He was asking me to submit to him in front of someone else.

I've been thinking about it a lot and I've come to realize it's sort of like taking your wedding vows in front of someone. It was affirming in a way. A way of connecting somehow. I don't know if he had such romantic notions or just wanted me to show my garters, but slowly I lifted my skirt, my face hot, with another sort of fire starting a slow burn inside of me as well.

George whistled softly and I tried to hide a smile. He was so different from my formal Mr. Stevenson. "Sensational," he breathed. "May I see more?"

"Certainly," Mr. Stevenson said calmly, as if I were a piece of meat or a swath of fabric. "Take off your skirt and blouse, Olivia."

Just like that. Take off your clothes. Well, lifting my skirt was one thing. But take it all off? I rebelled inside though I didn't say anything. No protesting, just a little fight in my head. After all, I'd already lifted the skirt. It was a matter of degree, wasn't it? I'd already admitted through my actions that I was Mr. Stevenson's slut. His slave.

Just writing the words. His slave. What does that mean? I don't know, but I get shivers just writing it. I looked up suddenly and Mr. Stevenson was staring at me. He didn't look angry or demanding. He just looked expectant and proud. Yes, that was it. He looked proud and happy that I belonged to him, and he was showing his old friend that I did.

Somehow, that made me feel proud too. Perhaps if he'd been all stern and angry-looking I would have rebelled, but instead, I found myself wanting to please him. To earn the pride he clearly felt. Slowly, I reached behind and unzipped the skirt, letting it fall.

My blouse buttoned in back and I had a little trouble with it, but they were watching intently, neither one looking impatient. I let it fall and stood there, not sure what to do with my hands, resisting my initial impulse to cover myself, knowing Mr. Stevenson wouldn't want that.

"Take off the brassiere, Olivia." My hands were trembling, but somehow I got all those stupid hooks open. I felt the air cool against my bare nipples. Now impulse overcame obedience and I covered myself.

"Drop your arms, slave."

Slave.

I did, slowly lowering my arms, standing taller. I was wearing nothing but my panties, stockings and garters, with my heels still on as well. I felt like one of those cheesecake poster girls my dad had in his garage when I was a kid.

I do have nice breasts, if a little small, and my legs aren't bad either. I'm one of the lucky girls who didn't age overnight from childbirth, like so many of my friends. I couldn't figure out what to do with my hands, so I just let them fall to my sides.

They were both staring now. Mr. Stevenson had a slight enigmatic smile on his face, but George was just plain gaping. I don't think he's married, but surely he's seen a woman's breasts before! His eyes were kind of glazed and his hand dropped down to his trousers, perhaps to hide the obvious bulge there.

I felt so strange. At once embarrassed and excited. That combination seems to be happening a lot lately. I stood there waiting, wondering what was coming next and if I would have the "grace" as Mr. Stevenson says, to submit to it.

"Go to the wall, Olivia," Mr. Stevenson said, his voice quiet but commanding. "Forehead against it, ass out." We'd done this before. A very humiliating position, like a schoolgirl waiting for punishment in those old Victorian novels. It was one thing to do it for Mr. Stevenson. But knowing George was watching made it that much more intense.

Slowly I walked to the wall, almost in a daze. I pressed my forehead against the cold, hard surface and stuck my bottom out. My legs were trembling, which was annoying on my wobbly high heels. As if reading my mind, Mr. Stevenson said, "Take off your shoes, Olivia. You'll need your balance."

I slipped them off, pondering the meaning of those words. I was soon to find out what he meant. "Hands in front of you. Clasp them together, and don't let go, no matter what." I obeyed, finding the position somewhat difficult with my forehead still pressed against the wall. I felt more silly than sexy, except for that hot pit of yearning now boiling up inside of me as I considered my position in front of these men!

Mr. Stevenson addressed George and what he said almost made me turn around and bolt right out of there. But I didn't! I stayed right where I was, now glad my face was hidden from them, as he said, "My slave girl sometimes requires a good spanking. It keeps her in line and reminds her of her place."

Oh, my God. In front of George! I felt my face burning so hot my ears actually stung! I heard George comment, "She's got a great ass, James. Just made for spanking. You are one lucky devil. Think I could give it a try?"

"Certainly. But not right away. I'll get her warmed up first."

Now, that wasn't part of the deal! Hadn't he said I wouldn't be expected to do anything sexual with Mr. Hawkins? But was a spanking sexual? I was confused and nervous, but excited as usual. I could hear Mr. Stevenson coming up behind me and I felt his large firm hands against my bottom. He cupped the cheeks, lifting them and letting them fall. I knew George was watching.

Smack! Mr. Stevenson slapped my bottom, starting out hard right away. No easing into it. He hit me hard! Maybe he wanted to impress George with what I would take for him. I let out a very unladylike little grunt when he did that, not expecting him to lay into me like that!

"Stay still! Show your grace!" he hissed in my ear. I realized this wasn't just about me now. He wanted to impress his buddy.

I tried to stay still as he smacked one cheek and then the other, hard as you like, until I was panting and gripping my hands hard to keep from reaching back and pushing him away. It was very difficult to keep my position and my forehead kept slipping from the wall and then getting bumped with the impact of his palm against my bottom. My back was starting to hurt from arching out like that. I felt ungraceful and awkward and wished he would stop!

Well, he did stop, only to say, "Would you like a hand at it, George?"

I honestly don't think I could have taken anymore. I was on the verge of protest but George said, "I would. God, yes. But James, I'd like her over my lap. Would that be all right, do you think?"

At least I'd get to lie down! Get out of this awkward position. I expected Mr. Stevenson to order me to the couch. But he surprised me by whispering into my ear, "Would you permit that, Olivia? It's beyond our agreement for today. To lie on his lap, I mean. If you're not comfortable with that, I completely understand."

I guess I was so surprised at being asked my permission that I found myself nodding and murmuring that it would be fine. Then I thought to add, "But I don't think I can take much more, Sir!" I rubbed my cheeks, feeling the heat emanating from them, knowing they must be bright cherry red.

Aloud Mr. Stevenson said, "Olivia agrees that you may spank her over your lap, George. She is submitting to me in this regard because she belongs to me. I would ask though that you be gentler than I was, since she's nearing her limit."

I draped myself over the smaller man, feeling incredibly sexy now. I felt like some special, rare orchid, the way they were discussing my submissive nature and how I "belonged" to Mr. Stevenson and needed to be treated gently. It seems odd to write this, but this is what I experienced!

His hands were on me now, not cool and firm like Mr. Stevenson, but kind of damp and floppy. He must have been nervous. Mr. Stevenson and I have built something up over months but poor little George was just plopped right down in the middle of it! Not that he was suffering unduly, I wouldn't think. At first, he was more massaging than spanking me. I got the feeling that he was just so thrilled to be touching a woman.

After a while, though, his hand became firmer, smacking the flesh already made tender by Mr. Stevenson. I began to move beneath him, unable to stay still. I began to gasp, small, yelping sounds with each smack. He pressed his hand firmly against the small of my back, which somehow calmed me, though I found I could barely get my breath.

"She's so responsive," he murmured, which both embarrassed and pleased me.

When his hand strayed down between my legs, which had fallen apart during the spanking, I slammed them together, shocked at his presumption, which is kind of funny, when you think about it.

Luckily, Mr. Stevenson must have been watching because he said, "That's enough now, I think, George. Olivia's had enough. Let her up."

He did, thank goodness, and I stood rather too quickly. The blood rushed from my head and I swayed, black spots in front of my eyes for a few seconds. I felt Mr. Stevenson's strong arms around me.

He murmured, "You were wonderful. Take your things and get dressed. Then come back to us, dear. We'll be waiting."

chapter IO

TESS WAS SPRAWLED across Brad's bed, one hand partially covering her face. Her dark wavy hair spread over the pillow. Brad had covered his nude lover with a light quilt, but one breast was exposed, the nipple a pretty pink against soft, creamy skin. A breeze from the open window stirred the curtains and Tess shifted but didn't awaken.

Brad stood awhile admiring the lovely girl. His need for coffee got the better of him, however, and he headed to the kitchen to make some. As he measured the beans and ground them, he lost himself in pleasant daydreams.

Until Tess had entered his life, Brad had prided himself on being impervious when it came to the wiles of women. Sure, he dated but invariably it wasn't long before he was bored at best, desperate to escape at worst. He'd even had a few serious relationships, two of them lasting more than a year before he finally admitted that the bloom was off the rose.

If he were honest, the seeds of his discontent were usually planted early, but he would dismiss or ignore them, willing things to be perfect despite evidence to the contrary.

Yet with Tess things were different and had been from the start. Even before the wonderful overlay of D/s was added to their developing relationship, there had been no false moves, no double takes at some remark she made or action she did that would ring false somewhere in his psyche. Tess was so different from his usual women.

In the past, he had found himself drawn to what he thought of as dark women. Women who were mysterious and perhaps somewhat inaccessible. A challenge. He would set his sights on such a woman, determined to claim to her for his own. Yet invariably, what started out as mystery and a challenge ended up devolving into something less than satisfying.

Tess was different. He was always learning something new and wonderful when he was with her, not only about her, but about himself. He loved her optimism and her zest for experience. Most of all, he loved her passion.

Though he felt foolish to admit it now, when he'd first agreed to have dinner with her, he had just viewed her as a diversion. When she'd stuck her pretty head in his office door with the casual offer of dinner at a restaurant, he had quickly assessed the potential fun factor and decided to go for it.

He'd had her pegged as a sweet, little do-gooder—probably a little boring in the sack, but that would be compensated for by her fantastic body and obvious eagerness. He'd avoided becoming intimate right away as a calculated ploy to get her desire up. Women were so easy. He'd always had the knack of withholding what they most wanted until it was all they could think of. And then, when he provided it, they would invariably fall head over heels.

What he hadn't counted on was Tess herself. Her complexity, coupled with her honest willingness and open joy in exploring their newfound D/s relationship with him, kept him slightly off-balance. While he wasn't looking, she had somehow slipped into his heart. And yet, he found he liked being off-kilter, if that was what it was. He liked being constantly and pleasantly surprised by what Tess wanted and was willing to do.

Last night had been amazing. The thrill of the power of having the naked, lovely young woman tied and bound, completely at his mercy, was electrifying. Even now, his cock responded to the memory, stirring in his underwear as he saw Tess's head falling back, her eyes closed, her lips parted and glistening, her body covered in a sheen of sweat, her nipples dark red and engorged. He could almost hear the sweet moan as the whip's lash caught her flesh.

At first, he had been afraid of hurting her. Of moving from the erotic pleasure of pain to something that was dangerous, or no longer pleasurable for Tess. But she had led him, in her quiet and sexy way, giving clear cues that she wanted what he was offering. Wanted it and more. By the end of the flogging, Brad's cock was rock-hard and dripping as he watched his lover swaying in her bonds, moaning and sighing, sounding as if she were climaxing just from the stinging kiss of his whip.

When he'd finally entered her, it was all he could do to keep from ejaculating immediately. The flogging had been extended foreplay, wildly stimulating to both of them. The thrill and intensity of the experience had opened his eyes to what sex could be. His imaginative mind was already outlining scenarios including his submissive girl, lots of naughty toys and himself as lord and master.

Brad was shaken out of his reverie when he heard the sound of the electric garage door opening. Peter wasn't due back until the next day. Brad panicked for a moment, thinking of the chains still hanging from the ceiling and the flogger lying where it had been dropped. He had planned to remove the hooks, use spackling and a dab of paint on the ceiling, removing all the evidence before his roommate returned.

It wasn't that he was necessarily trying to hide the evidence—it just wasn't any of Peter's business. While Brad stood uncertain, clad only in black boxer shorts, his roommate opened the garage door and came into the kitchen.

Peter, who stood at six-foot five, was long-limbed and narrow. He sometimes reminded Brad of a praying mantis, especially when he unfolded himself from a chair or car that was too small for him. His face was long and thin with a hawkish nose, and almost lugubrious, with droopy eyes that gave him a hangdog look.

For all that, the total package was attractive, with dark blond curly hair, worn long, making him look younger than his twenty-seven years and a wickedly acerbic sense of humor that appealed to his friends and irritated his enemies.

Now he breezed in, gave Brad a once-over and said, "Finally brought her here, huh? About time! When do I get to meet the gorgeous attorney with the legs that don't quit and the breasts that make grown men cry?"

"Shh, she'll hear you." Brad grinned, forgetting for a moment that the evidence of their BDSM play was in the next room. "She's sleeping, so keep it down. What are you doing here? You weren't due back till tomorrow."

"Thanks, it's great to see you too, pal." Peter grinned, but added, "The meeting tanked. I didn't want to waste my time with those idiots. They had no business plan and no clear idea of what they were doing. Worse, I suspect some book cooking."

Peter was a venture capital guy, who found promising companies and helped them package themselves to get loans and capital. He was just coming into his stride and saving a nice nest egg to buy a house for himself and his girl.

"Anyway," he shrugged his overnight bag off his shoulder, "I'm hungry. What you got there?" He shook his head dismissively when Brad held up a loaf of bread and nodded toward the toaster. "I need food, buddy! Maybe I'll make some pancakes. You up for that?"

Brad, who was always up for Peter's cooking, nodded. Peter leaned into the refrigerator, pulling out milk and eggs. "Ah, and these strawberries should do nicely. A little on the ripe side, but perfect for pancakes. How about Tess? Does she eat?" Peter's girlfriend was on a constant diet, a source of frustration to Peter, who regarded himself as something of a gourmet cook.

"Like a horse!" Brad laughed, thinking fondly of his darling girl, whose slender frame belied her love of food, and lots of it. "I'll go see if she wants something." He decided to make a quick detour, at least collecting the whip and spreader bar. Maybe Peter wouldn't notice the chains, and if he did, so what. It was Brad's house, after all. He could do as he liked.

He hurried from the kitchen, leaving his roommate to his preparations. He was just heading out of the exercise room, his arms full of the toys, when he collided in the hall with Peter. It was so unexpected that Brad swore, dropping the items and stumbling for a moment to get his balance.

"Whoa, sorry there, my brother," Peter said. He leaned down automatically to help Brad with the things he'd dropped. Then he realized what he was handling. "Holy shit! What the hell is this, Brad? And what's this thing?" He lifted the spreader bar, as Brad snatched it from him, blushing furiously, and doubly angry at himself for the blush.

"Gimme that!" Brad said, reaching for the flogger in Peter's other hand. Peter held it higher, out of Brad's reach, doing a little jig in the hall. "Come on, Peter. Cut it out. It's just a few sex toys. No big deal. We were just having some fun." He tried to pull the exercise room door shut, but Peter edged past him and stepped in. As he took in the chains and cuffs dangling from the ceiling, the grin widened across his narrow face.

"Brad Hunter, you old devil! Just what in the hell were you two perverts up to last night? Is this what you do at her house? What is she, some kind of Elvira Dominatrix all dressed up in a patent-leather jumpsuit and stiletto heels? Holy shit! I had no idea you were into that stuff, Brad! All these years we've known each other, and I never knew you were a subby boy into getting whipped by his nasty little Mistress!"

Brad's lips were pressed in a thin line and his eyes were flashing. But Peter looked so goofy, grinning and waving the whip, his eyes twinkling with suppressed glee, that Brad couldn't help but laugh a little himself. Why did he have to hide it, anyway? What he and Tess had shared had been breathtaking. It had been consensual and romantic and certainly more intense than any "straight" experience he'd ever had.

His face became serious and he said quietly, "Peter, it's the most amazing thing I've ever experienced. Come make us some pancakes and I'll tell you a little about it."

When Tess came into the kitchen wrapped in Brad's silk robe, her hair sweetly tousled and her face still pink with sleep, the two men were at the table, drinking their second cups of coffee, the evidence of stacks of pancakes just a sticky puddle of buttery syrup on their plates. They stopped their conversation, turning their heads toward her.

"Oh," Tess said, pulling the robe more tightly around her.

Brad jumped up, feeling guilty he had forgotten to warn Tess that Peter had returned. He put his arm around her and kissed the top of her head. "Tess. This is Peter, my roommate. He came back earlier than expected. He's made us pancakes as a peace offering."

Peter stood, towering over the young woman, his sad-eyed face creased in a large grin. Brad had filled him in on the aspects of their unique relationship, and Peter had been awed, impressed and very curious.

He kissed Tess's hand, which made her giggle, and inclined his head in a regal bow. "You are far lovelier than even Brad was able to convey. Welcome to our humble abode. It's a pleasure to meet you."

_*_

Tess hadn't wanted to share her morning with a stranger, but Peter was charming, and she was hungry. Reading her mind, Peter dropped her hand, heading toward the counter. "I saved you some batter. I'll just whip up a plate of hotcakes for you, mademoiselle, and Brad here will serve your coffee."

Tess liked that fine. She sat down at the table, enjoying having the two men wait on her. Brad kept her company as she ate, while Peter went off to shower and change. After she'd put away four pancakes and was sipping a second cup of hot coffee with fresh cream, Brad said, "Tess. He came so unexpectedly. And he saw the stuff. He knows."

Tess's stomach lurched for a moment with dread. Peter knew about their secret games! Her first impulse was to grab her clothes and run out of there. Brad, watching her, put his hand on her arm and gave it a gentle squeeze.

"Relax. He's totally cool with it. In fact, he's more than cool, he's fascinated. He actually told me he's always had an interest in the idea of erotic submission. He even admitted he'd playfully tried to get Amy to let him tie her up, but she wasn't going for it. I'm just telling you this so you can relax.

"And anyway, Tess. Isn't this more to us than a game now? Why should we have to hide it from people who matter to us? I know society at large might not understand what we share now, but that doesn't make it less valid, or less right for us.

"Tell me honestly—" he stroked a finger along Tess's cheek. "Wasn't last night amazing? Was it just me, or did you feel an intense connection like nothing we've achieved before? You truly submitted to me last night, Tess. And it was what I wanted. What I longed for."

Tess nodded. "It was beyond amazing. It was the most intense thing I've ever experienced! I want to experience that erotic intensity with you again and again. I long for it too. I dreamt about it all night. God, Brad. Whatever's happening here, do you want it to continue?"

"More than anything, Tess. You are so fucking hot. I want you on your knees in front of me, ready to do whatever I ask of you. Do you want that?"

Tess nodded, smiling shyly. She laughed a little, and said, "I was even thinking of just that! Of coming into the kitchen and kneeling in front of you. Asking for a little protein, if you know what I mean. Peter being there though, that just kind of threw me off! That and these delicious pancakes! The dude can cook!"

They laughed but then they both got serious again. Brad said, "Tess. This is something I want you to think about. I mean, this whole thing of submission. I want to take it beyond the games, beyond the fooling around. But I don't want to rush you. I think you are incredibly sexy and naturally submissive, but I also know I can be pretty damn pushy, and this is not something that should be forced. Not ever."

Tess looked at him, her demeanor serious. "I never thought I would ever really act on what you are calling my submissive feelings. I don't know if I, the successful young attorney, would have been able to reconcile my submissive sexual needs with my own image of myself as a modern, liberated woman. And yet, with your help, I think I'm coming to realize how incredibly liberating—yes—that's the word! How liberating it is to acknowledge and embrace these feelings. I feel so alive, and so, well, this may sound weird, but so brave! Like we're exploring a whole new world together. Though, obviously, it's been explored before.

"Whatever Olivia and I share—remember she called it a secret language? Well, you and I speak it too, don't we, Brad? And it's weird, how her journal has paralleled what we're discovering. Though it's sad too. For her, I mean."

"Yes, it is sad, in some regard," Brad agreed. "She could never tell anyone. And she could never truly consummate the submission with Mr. Stevenson. He was, after all, her boss. A married man, and she a married woman. It's amazing that they were doing all that wild stuff during the workday, and then she'd go home and make macaroni and cheese and take the kids to the dentist or for a carriage ride or whatever people did back then."

"Come on, Brad, it wasn't that long ago!"

"I'm teasing, silly. Just think, they started this thing in 1961. Your nana was one of the first liberated women, part of the sexual revolution that would change the world."

Tess thought a minute and offered, "You know, I think if I'd found those diaries without having met you, without having explored these feelings within myself, I probably would have shrugged off her affair as just some sordid office fling. Though admittedly not a typical one, with whips and rulers, and exposing yourself for clients! But I wouldn't have seen it as brave or liberating. Now I understand. She was an amazing woman, my Nana."

"She was, and so are you. Just as sexy, submissive, brave and courageous as Olivia was. You're opening yourself to understand what you truly are. And you're helping me to do the same. Maybe we're becoming, together, what we were always meant to be."

Tess nodded, feeling gratitude and pleasure in equal measure. "My God, Brad, you've summed it up so beautifully. Just right. That's exactly it. Thank you." And, kneeling before him, she kissed his feet. It felt natural and burningly correct. When he pulled her up into his arms, their lips met and the fire seared into each of them.

chapter II

January 5, 1962

WELL, HAPPY NEW Year. Christmas break was wonderful of course, but a part of me was longing to get back to work. I felt guilty about it and really tried to focus on the family. But there you are.

I guess a new year brings new things. Beware what you say you'll never do. It usually comes back to bite you in the rear. I never thought I'd put my mouth on a man's thing. A man's penis. Mr. Stevenson says I shouldn't be shy about using the right words. Though he doesn't say penis—he calls it his "cock".

"Today," he told me Wednesday, "will be a test of your submission. You are going to suck my cock. You are going to learn the art of fellatio." Fellatio! It sounds like a character in an Italian opera. But that's not what it is. He expects me to get on my knees, to open his pants, pull out his penis and put my mouth on it!

And that's not all! I am supposed to learn to please him until his "release". He is going to come in my mouth!

I can't do it! I tell you, I can't do it. I won't do it. It isn't natural!

I told him so and he smiled that slow lazy smile of his. "Olivia, who do you belong to?"

I admit it—I love when he says that. There's something so sexy and intense about it. And the way he says it, so soft and low, like a caress.

"You, Sir," I whispered.

"Then how can you refuse me? Do you understand when you refuse something I want you are saying, through your actions, that you don't trust me? That you don't belong to me at all. That you are just playacting to satisfy your own sexual whims?"

I just looked at him. He's right, you know. I love the game, as long as it's my rules we're playing by. I can pretend to be "submissive" all I want but when he does ask me to do things that I find abhorrent or frightening, I balk.

I know people do it. Prostitutes do it for money. I'm sure many married women do it for their husbands. I've certainly never known anyone who did, or any man who asked for it for that matter! But then again, maybe I do know these people and just don't know it. It's not something you would advertise, obviously. I think it's against the law in most states.

But you really don't know things about people, do you? No matter how well you think you know them. I'm obvious living proof of that! Betty and Marie would never dream of what goes on at my office. How do I know what goes on in their bedrooms—or out of them, for that matter?

Mr. Stevenson didn't press me right away, thank goodness. He said he'd give me time to think about it. He said he wanted me to come to him and ask to suck his cock. Beg to suck it. To prove my desire to truly submit to him. To allow myself to move to a higher plane of submission.

Sometimes I think he's full of soup. He puts these ideas in my head and couches them in lofty sentiment, just to get what he wants! For free too. I bet Mrs. Stevenson wouldn't be caught dead with his "cock" in her mouth!

January 7, 1962

He has this way of working on me. Subtly. Like this latest thing, that I'm to come to him. I'm to ask him for permission to take his member into my mouth! But now, perversely, I find I can't stop thinking about it! What would it taste like? Would it be pissy? Yeech! Just the thought is nauseating! It's unsanitary!

What would it feel like? Of course, I've felt a penis. They are soft on the outside—soft and smooth while being nice and hard underneath. But I've never felt one with my tongue! Frank would die before he'd ask me to take his penis into my mouth. If I ever asked him to let me do that, he'd probably divorce me flat out.

But Mr. Stevenson not only wants it, he wants me to beg for it.

To beg for it.

_*_

January 14, 1962

It wasn't so bad! I did it. I know, I feel like such a total slut. And yet, the feeling isn't a bad one. It's sexy. And not only that, I feel empowered somehow. I was able to draw a response from Mr. Stevenson that is rare. For that moment, he was the one who was out of control. It was exciting. I think I had a glimpse of what it must feel like to dominate another. To take control, to reduce someone to pure lust and need. To know you are the one creating that in them.

It wasn't really disgusting at all. He says I'll need practice. Much more practice. He says now that I've properly submitted by begging to take it, he can teach me at a slower pace to properly service his cock. His words.

Here's what happened, as best as I can relate it. I'd been obsessing, yes, that's the only word, about his damn penis and how he expected me to lick it and suck it. We went through a whole week and he didn't mention it, except obliquely, questioning if I was ready to submit properly or if I needed another spanking or time in the corner to think things over.

Oddly, I do some good thinking when I'm forced into the corner, my skirt lifted, my face pressed into the wall. It's not comfortable but it's very erotic. Erotic discomfort, Mr. Stevenson calls it. I feel very submissive, very vulnerable, in that position.

I was in that corner, thinking about his cock and wondering if I could actually do what he wanted. I decided I was being foolish in resisting. And not only that, I was curious now. Very curious what it would be like and if I could handle it.

When he released me, I said, "Sir. I think I'm ready."

"Ready?" He looked genuinely puzzled.

"To, um, you know. Your penis."

The bastard forced me to be "articulate". "I don't understand," he said, offering a faint smile. I knew he understood perfectly well, but it's part of the humiliation to make me say it. To make me say things that make me blush.

"I...um...want to suck your penis, Sir."

Now he actually grinned. "Well, that's good to hear, slave. It's only taken you a week longer than it should have. The moment I first asked you, you should have dropped to your knees and opened your mouth. But I'm glad you've come to it at last."

I expected him to open his pants but he walked around to his desk and said, "Go work at your desk. When I'm ready for your, uh, services, I'll let you know."

Oh! That was classic Mr. Stevenson. After I'd finally worked up the nerve to ask, he'd sent me away to wait! Anticipation is key, he'd say. Timing, I suppose, is everything. As I sat at my desk, trying to work, I could barely sit still. I stuck a hand in my panties, feeling the hot wetness of my own sex. I rubbed a little and it felt good. Maybe I'd go into the bathroom, as I've taken to doing lately, when I can't concentrate on my work and just rub myself a little until I could calm down.

He chose that moment to call me in.

"Olivia."

I pulled my hand out of my panties, afraid for a second he'd seen me. I hurried in, very nervous but excited. Mr. Stevenson was standing in the middle of the room. His jacket was off but he was otherwise fully clothed.

"Kneel before me, slave," he intoned. I did so, feeling that lovely net of submissive release that seems to come over me when we play our games.

"Open my belt and my pants." I did, feeling somewhat awkward there on the ground. I managed to unbuckle the soft leather belt, and unbutton and unzip his pants. He pulled his shirt and undershirt out of the way, revealing his sensible white boxers. He pulled them down himself and out popped his large, hard cock!

It looked ridiculously large, now that I knew I was going to take it in my mouth! He just looked down at me. I had been expecting precise directions. He does love to direct. But all he said was, "Go ahead."

I squeezed my eyes shut and stuck my tongue out in the general direction of his penis. I could smell it. It wasn't stinky or anything, thank God! It was more of a spicy scent, I guess you could say. And a hint of soap. My tongue made contact with the spongy head, and I licked across it, my eyes still shut.

"For God's sake, Olivia. You look like you're tasting a lemon or something much worse! It's only a penis, for heaven's sake. Stop acting like a silly girl!" Chagrined, I opened my eyes and tried again. I licked around the head, as it bobbed toward me. I dared to take the base of it in my hand, to keep it steady. It was surprisingly hot to the touch, and I actually felt it harden even further under my hand.

But it was my mouth he wanted and I licked down the underside, which was smooth and satiny. He sighed a little and closed his eyes so I figured I was on the right track. I licked around to the front and felt the bulging vein throbbing against my mouth.

"Yes," he murmured. He took my head in his hands and guided himself partially into my mouth. I pulled back, panicking. I couldn't take that thing in my mouth! But he held my head and whispered, "Relax, darling. You can do this. Do it for me. Relax and open your throat and be calm and joyous in the knowledge that you're pleasing me."

His voice, his words. As usual, they struck some perfect resonant chord in me and I actually felt my muscles relaxing, my pulse slowing. I stayed still, kneeling there at his feet as he slid that huge erection past my lips.

He moaned, moving his penis in and out of my mouth. I tried to kiss and lick the shaft as it moved in and out and I reached down and cupped the heavy balls. They felt so delicate, like robin's eggs nestled in the soft, loose flesh.

It was weird, because I'm used to being the one that loses control at his hand. The one moaning with pleasure or pain or the delicious combination of the two. But now it was he, my "Master", his body stiff and arching, his moans sweet and low with passion.

I'll admit here, I started to panic when I could tell he was about to climax. The thought of him ejaculating into my mouth was—is—so disgusting that I knew I'd end up gagging—spitting it out and making a scene. I'd ruin what was a very sexy and intense moment by spitting up like a baby. He must have sensed my tension in the rigidity of my body because he whispered urgently, "Relax, beautiful girl! I won't come in your mouth. Not this time. Just take it! Just as you are—don't stop!"

He held my head tightly now and fucked my face, no other words for it. I felt a curious tightening in his balls and suddenly he pulled away, spurting his copious seed into his own hand, as he fell to his knees, his pants around his ankles.

I sat there, my mouth still open, as he slumped back, his face twisted in orgasmic pleasure, his hand still cupped. After a moment or two, he recovered himself, though he was still flushed. He looked like such a sweet mess, disheveled and exposed. Defenseless in his own orgasm, for that one moment no one's master.

He smiled at me, his expression so tender I was taken aback. He leaned close to me and bringing his head down to mine, he kissed my neck. He whispered so I could barely hear, but I swear he said, "I love you."

chapter 12

Tess closed the last of the notebooks. Was this all there was? Surely there were more packed away somewhere! They would have to tear apart that attic.

Tess found herself wondering for days about it. Were there other pale blue booklets filled with Olivia's neat, precise hand, lying about waiting to be discovered? Or was that all she wrote? A very thorough search of Nana's attic did not disgorge any more secret diaries, alas, and Tess was left to speculate on her own.

Did Olivia and Mr. Stevenson move from their little games into something more serious? Did Olivia know instinctively that, while it was one thing to write about the games, it was another to document a real love affair? Perhaps those last words said all that needed to be said.

Tess sighed. She would never know. Nana was gone and so were her secrets. Not that Tess would have asked! Or would she?

_*_

Later that day found Tess and Brad back at Nana's house, finishing the last of the packing and sorting. She looked around the familiar old place, sighing. The furniture would be picked up later in the week and the place would be put up for sale. Tess had brought Brad with her for moral support, and also so he could get a sense of what her grandmother's home had been like.

As he took in the old-fashioned rattan furniture, the homespun braided throw rugs and the Norman Rockwells on the wall, he grinned. "Who would ever have suspected? The secret, smoldering, submissive passion behind all this bric-a-brac!" He pointed toward one of Nana's many cross-stitched homilies, nestled on the wall between old pictures of her children when they were young, grinning gap-toothed shy smiles for the camera.

Tess was about to comment when the phone rang. She turned toward it. "Now who could that be? Maybe my mom with more last-minute instructions."

"Hello?"

There was a pause during which Tess almost hung up and then a hesitant voice, though deep and resonant, and familiar said, "Tess? Is this Tess Shepard?"

"Why, yes. Who is this?" Tess's heart had begun to pound. Even as her conscious mind hadn't quite processed who was on the phone, she knew. She recognized the voice from that single word she'd heard those several weeks before, when he'd said, "Olivia." That single-word command, her grandmother had referenced so many times in her journals.

"This is James Stevenson. I knew your grandmother."

"Mr. Stevenson! Hello." Brad looked up from wrapping the framed photograph he was holding and come to stand near Tess.

"I hope you don't mind my calling you. I actually spoke to your mother, who told me I might find you at Olivia's place. I feel terrible I wasn't here for the funeral. I was out of the country. I—I called because Olivia spoke of you fondly and often."Tess warmed at this statement and her eyes filled with tears.

"I thought maybe, if we talked." Mr. Stevenson hesitated. "I don't know. I think I'm trying to say I need some kind of closure though to be perfectly honest I'm feeling like a bit of a fool right now. We—we were very close, your grandmother and I."

What an understatement, Tess thought, suppressing a smile. He sounded so formal, yet Tess could sense the deep sadness beneath his words and the longing for some connection, however small, to his once-beloved Olivia.

On a whim, Tess offered, "Mr. Stevenson. Would you like to meet for dinner? I'd love to hear your memories of my grandmother. You worked together many years. I could share stories about her too. It might be a beginning of closure for both of us."

"That would be wonderful. In fact, you took the words out of my mouth."

"I'd like to bring my," Tess hesitated, not sure how to refer to Brad, who was watching her, his head tilted, as if he could hear both sides of the conversation. "...y friend, Brad Hunter."

"Of course." They fixed the place and date for the coming Saturday evening and said their goodbyes.

She hung up and turned expectantly toward Brad. "Can you believe that? Mr. Stevenson, on the phone! And now we get to meet him."

"You have some nerve, Tess!" Brad laughed. "I'm almost scared at what comes next. Are you going to demand an explanation? Insist on knowing why he cuckolded your grandfather for all those years? Or are you going to ask for lessons? Become another apprentice in the art of submission?"

Tess lifted her eyebrows. "I would think you'd be the one asking for an apprenticeship, my dominant lover."

"Oh?" Brad took her in his arms. "Are you saying I need lessons? Come here, I'll show you what I've learned so far." Packing was forgotten as Brad claimed his lover on her grandmother's living room floor.

_*_

That Saturday night found Tess and Brad at Bennington's, a very fine upscale establishment chosen by Mr. Stevenson. Tess scanned the room as the maitre d' looked skeptically at his clipboard, shaking his head as if to say there was no possible way these two young people would be seated any time soon.

Tess ignored him completely, trying to determine if Mr. Stevenson had already arrived. She saw a very distinguished-looking man in his mid-seventies. His hair was silver, brushed back from a high forehead. His eyes were keen and bright blue—not faded with time as happened to some, and his face crinkled in a pleasant smile when he saw Tess and Brad. He raised a hand in greeting as they approached the table, leaving the maitre d' to scowl after them.

Rising, the old gentleman took Tess's hand and held it for a moment, smiling at her. "What a pleasure to meet you at last. Your grandmother spoke of you often." His eyes looked wet and he dropped her hand, clearly trying to compose himself.

Brad extended his hand. "A pleasure to meet you, Mr. Stevenson. I'm Brad Hunter. I never knew Olivia Winston personally, but somehow I feel as if I do. She and Tess are very much alike in some ways." Tess resisted an urge to punch him in the arm for that remark, full of its own hidden meaning.

"James Stevenson, at your service. And please, call me James."

They all sat and ordered drinks from the young man who hovered discreetly nearby. The evening began with small talk. Mr. Stevenson revealed that his own wife had died some three years before. He lived a quiet life, enjoying his solitude and taking pleasure in his grandchildren when they visited.

Tess found herself burning with the desire to question him, to tell him that they knew. That they had the journals. She kept staring at him, looking for evidence of the man Olivia had written about so passionately in her journals. His hands looked strong—the fingers long and tapered, the nails manicured. He was a very handsome man, much more so than her grandfather Frank had been. He must have been quite stunning as a younger man. Tess realized to her surprise that she was attracted to him! To a man, who had been her grandmother's lover.

The restaurant was fancy and of the old-school belief that the meal should be an event. They each had two drinks—Tess noted Mr. Stevenson still favored a martini with two olives—before the appetizer finally arrived. When the avocado lobster rolls with a spicy cilantro dipping sauce did finally appear, Tess found herself rather tipsy. Even at the best of times, she didn't hold her liquor well.

When the main meal was served, Mr. Stevenson ordered a fine champagne to toast their shared memories, he said. Tess could never resist champagne and despite her own awareness that she was getting quite drunk, she happily tilted the crystal flute and drank to her grandmother's memory.

Brad and Mr. Stevenson began to discuss the law and how being an attorney had changed from the sixties to now. Tess watched them both, looking up through thick lashes, having another glass of the bubbly champagne.

They were all going to dance around it, weren't they? They had talked freely for over an hour, but said very little of import. She and Brad knew this huge secret that had shaped her grandmother's life and surely had affected this debonair man sitting with them. And none of them were going to say a word!

It must have been the liquor that loosened her tongue, because the words slipped out before she could censor them. "We found the journals, you know. The secret diaries."

Brad stopped what he had been saying mid-sentence. They both turned to stare at her. Brad's expression was surprised, incredulous even, and overlain with a warning.

He put his hand over hers and said quietly, "Tess. You've had too much to drink."

Mr. Stevenson was also staring at her. At first, he didn't seem to understand, but then realization dawned on his face and he grew pale. Clutching his glass, he said quietly, "Her diaries? She still had them, after all these years?"

Tess let out her breath, now blushing hotly as the import of her admission struck her. She was dizzy and drank some cold water, trying to sort her muddled thoughts. Well, the cat was out of the bag now. No point in denying it.

"Yes," she whispered. "I found them, locked up discreetly in a little trunk in the attic. I'm sure no one but she had ever seen them."

"Until you, I suppose you mean? You read her secret, private journals?" Mr. Stevenson's tone was mild, bewildered.

Shamed pricked at Tess as Mr. Stevenson gazed at her quizzically. It was like peeking in on lovers who didn't know you were there. Tess had hesitated only briefly before opening the diaries, and then she had compounded her crime by sharing them with her lover.

Brad put a reassuring hand on Tess's arm. Turning to Mr. Stevenson, he said, "Let's put things in perspective. If you had discovered old tracts of writing buried in your relative's attic, wouldn't you have done the same? Tess loved her grandmother with all her heart. They were closer even than she and her own mother. Imagine being offered the chance, after someone you love has just died, to somehow connect with them again, however briefly, however illusory. A chance to perhaps know them a little better, for a little longer. Would you deny yourself that chance? Honestly?"

Mr. Stevenson released his grip on his glass and sat back. Using the fine linen napkin, he wiped his forehead and then took another drink of water. "Very well. You've made your point, counselor." He managed a smile. "I imagine you must be quite formidable in the courtroom."

Brad smiled, offering the slightest hint of a nod.

Mr. Stevenson continued to nod in slow, thoughtful way. Finally he said, "I never read them, you know. She kept that little pile of blue notebooks in her bottom drawer and I never, ever looked at them. I would see her, scribbling away furiously at the end of many a day.

"At first, I was the one who suggested she keep that diary. I thought it would be a way to process things that were new and strange for her. But it was she who kept it up for so long. I used to tease her sometimes. Suggest that she was keeping notes for a great novel she would someday publish. She would laugh and tell me to mind my own business. For a submissive, she could be pretty bossy." Mr. Stevenson looked down, his own cheeks pink now, as he realized what he had just admitted.

Brad said, "Look, Mr. Stevenson, uh, James. I know this must be difficult for you. Embarrassing to know that we are aware of some of your most private and intimate secrets. I want to assure you that we have no intention of exploiting those secrets, or of compromising you in any way. To prove to you our sincerity, I'm going to share a secret of ours."

Without looking at Tess, Brad continued. "This lovely young woman you see before you—" he gestured toward Tess, whose heart had suddenly begun to hammer as she awaited his words, knowing she couldn't stop him, "—belongs to me. Much like Olivia belonged to you. She is my submissive. She has given herself freely to me."

Mr. Stevenson stared, saying nothing. Slowly his eyes raked Tess and it felt as if he were lighting her on fire with his gaze. The giddiness produced by the champagne seemed to suddenly recede, and Tess found that her mouth was dry and there were butterflies in her stomach.

"Brad!" she whispered fiercely, and his hand closed more firmly over hers. If she was going to deny it, to claim now it had only been a game and she was nobody's "submissive", this was the time to do it. And yet, even through her embarrassment at having been revealed to this stranger, or perhaps partially because of it, Tess couldn't deny the sweet heat building in her pussy.

"Do you deny it?" Brad asked quietly, his voice a dare. Tess looked down, confusion and desire rendering her mute. "Answer me," he insisted. "Tell us both, Tess. Do you belong to me? Are you submissive to me? Or were we just playacting?"

Tess couldn't bring herself to raise her head, but quietly she said, "I am yours." To admit it, in front of a witness. Not someone like Peter, who thought it was only silly fun, but to admit what she was in front of a man who clearly understood the import of the admission. Tess felt almost faint, but also deeply excited in the pit of her belly.

"Have her prove it." Mr. Stevenson's voice was low. There was a different quality to it now that they had shared their "secrets". Tess felt its power. She recalled Olivia's description of that voice, how it could control and command just by its very timbre and tone. Even now, all these years later, he had the power to command.

"Yes," Brad said softly, the idea taking hold. "Yes."

"Of course," Mr. Stevenson went on. "We are in a public place. So you'll have to be discreet. I suggest something simple. A testament of her desire to please you, even if it costs her something. Something like her modesty, perhaps." His bright blue eyes were glinting now, and Tess looked away, confused by the feelings of arousal and by the knowledge that a man many years her senior was partially the cause of it.

"A good suggestion, Sir," Brad said, his grin devilish. "Tess. Take off your panties and give them to Mr. Stevenson."

"Brad!" Tess was truly shocked! She had in fact been expecting something along these lines—perhaps being told to unbutton her blouse a bit, or go to the bathroom and bring Brad her underwear. But the added command to give her panties to this man! And to take them off right here? At the table?

Tess was dressed in a silky summer dress, which buttoned up the front and came in a full pretty skirt to just above her knees. As it was summer, she wore no stockings, and it would be rather simple to remove her panties under the table, draped as it was with heavy linen.

Mr. Stevenson's eyes sparkled and he smiled widely. "An excellent idea, Brad. How lucky you are, to have such an obedient and lovely submissive, and no need to hide it from the world."

Tess sat mute and unmoving. "Do you have a problem with what I'm asking, Tess? Is this too difficult for you? Are you refusing this very simple request?" Brad was still smiling, but now his eyes were sparked and flinty. She was testing him in front of another dominant. It was no longer strictly between them as lovers.

Reaching down, he slipped his hand under her dress and into her panties. His hard finger slid up her slit and he felt her wetness—ascertaining for himself the evidence of her desire, despite her lack of obedience at the moment.

Tess averted her face as Mr. Stevenson's intense gaze seemed to penetrate the heavy tablecloth. Tess wanted at once to disappear and to revel forever in the hot, sweet humiliation of the moment. Again, Brad asked her if she were refusing.

Quietly she demurred, "No, Sir." The "Sir" had slipped out, but felt natural on her tongue. Looking around the room, satisfying herself that no one was observing them, she lifted her bottom a little and slid her panties, embarrassingly damp now, down her smooth tan thighs. She reached under the table, holding her hand out to the older man.

"Here," she said, her voice trembling.

"No," said Brad. "Not under the table. Over it, so I can see. Let me watch you give your panties to this gentleman."

Face burning, Tess handed the little wadded-up offering to Mr. Stevenson. He took it, clasping her small hand in his large one for a moment as their eyes locked. Tess was the first to turn away. Mr. Stevenson slipped the panties in his suit jacket and patted it, smiling broadly at Brad.

"I wonder if it's genetic," he mused now, sipping at hot fragrant coffee.

"What's that?" Brad asked, taking a bite of his chocolate mousse. Tess sat there between them, still burning, while they chatted on about her as if she wasn't there or as if she were an object.

"This penchant for submission. This desire to be sensually controlled and subjected to sexual torture."

"An excellent question," Brad said expansively as he leaned back, lacing his fingers across his stomach like some old-time politician. "Olivia and now Tess. And perhaps the intervening generation as well, though of course, we aren't privy to that. Here we have these two women related by blood, longing to be controlled. To be used, and whipped and forced to do whatever their lord and master wants of them. To submit sexually to the whims of another."

"You could say the same about dominant impulses," Tess blurted, her own submissive feelings suddenly receding as they analyzed her in this clinical fashion.

"So you could," Mr. Stevenson laughed. "Touché, my dear. Though you should learn to curb your tongue. I know it's a new generation, but really, Brad, you might want to invest in a gag. They come in quite handy when your slave girl's tongue waggles too freely."

Brad laughed and Tess resisted her urge to kick him under the table. Their relationship wasn't like that! And yet, perhaps it only wasn't like that yet. They'd really only just begun to explore the power of dominance and submission, the heady potential of bondage and discipline. Who knew where it would take them, or how it would alter their interactions as lovers?

Tess took a spoonful of her raspberry sorbet, savoring its velvet sweetness on her tongue. What a twist of fate that she had met the man of Nana's dreams. They finished their desserts in companionable silence. Mr. Stevenson insisted on paying the bill though Tess protested that she had been the one to invite him.

"Next time, my dear," he said, smiling. "This way I can hope for a next time."

chapter 13

THEY LAY TOGETHER naked on the bed, their bodies entwined. The night was hot, but the air conditioning dried the sweat left from their lovers' dance, and Tess shivered in Brad's darkened bedroom. Sleepily, Brad caressed her breast, murmuring drowsily.

But Tess wasn't sleepy. She kept thinking about their conversation earlier in the evening, before Brad had tied her spread-eagled to the bed with long, thick leather straps and made delicious love to her until she cried for mercy.

He had told her that he had been in communication with Mr. Stevenson. Their dinner had been over a week before, and they had talked for several days about that night, about the journals, and about Mr. Stevenson's sudden entrance into their lives. For Tess, that had been it. She hadn't really thought beyond that dinner. Mr. Stevenson was still something less than real to her, she supposed. Meeting him in the flesh had just seemed like a finishing touch to the journals, something to make them more real.

But as they had parted that evening, he and Brad had exchanged cards. Brad's listed his status as an attorney, citing his law firm and work address, phone number, email address and website, while Mr. Stevenson's simply had his name, elegantly embossed on creamy fine paperboard, with his phone number printed discreetly below it. Brad had pocketed the card while Mr. Stevenson and Tess had said their goodnights.

"I shall treasure this little token," Mr. Stevenson had said, his eyes twinkling as he patted his pocket. Tess had blushed and turned away, confused by her own reaction, at once embarrassed and aroused.

Tonight Brad had told Tess that he and Mr. Stevenson had spoken a number of times. Tess's first reaction was to be hurt. She realized she regarded the journals, since they were her grandmother's, and by extension Mr. Stevenson, as "hers". She chose to share these things with Brad, but he had no right to act without her!

"You talked to him without me? When? Why didn't you tell me?"

"I'm telling you now, sweetheart. Don't act so miffed, please. Remember your place." He'd playfully twisted her nipple but hard enough for her to squeak a little in pain. As always, the pain was instantly replaced with a white-hot fire in her belly.

Brad said, "James and I—"

"Oh, James, is it?" Tess again interrupted, unconsciously touching her other nipple, which now wanted twisting as well.

"Jesus, Tess. I am going to have to gag you, aren't I? Now please shut up and let me talk!" Tess made a sulky face while Brad continued. "James talked about his relationship with Olivia. More than what's in the journals. Apparently, there were quite a few more of those little blue books. I wonder what happened to them."

"Maybe Pop found them and freaked out," Tess suggested, though she didn't believe it. Pop was one of the most incurious men she had ever met.

"Well, whatever happened to her diaries, he told me they continued to see one another, even after she'd retired. They managed to keep their affair secret for over forty years. Neither of them ever hinted a word of any of it to their respective spouses, both of whom died without ever knowing."

"I wonder why they didn't get together after Pop died? They could have had a year together, really together."

"I asked him about it. He was vague. He danced around it really, but I gathered from what hints and comments he did drop, that they were both used to the arrangement, which after all, they'd maintained for some forty years! Maybe they thought they'd ruin whatever special thing they had if they changed the formula. And maybe they would have, who knows? Perhaps your grandmother didn't want the scandal of her family suddenly questioning why she was marrying her old boss. I don't really know. But they did continue to meet regularly at a hotel downtown, once a week, like clockwork."

"Wow. Do you think he'd talk to me about it? I'd love to know more."

"I doubt it. He doesn't strike me as the type who would kiss and tell. But beyond that, he really is old-fashioned when it comes to women. He thinks a submissive should be more seen than heard. I don't think he'd find it seemly, yes, that would be the word, to discuss his sexual liaisons with a young submissive woman. Especially his lover's granddaughter!"

"Huh." Tess understood, but still it irritated her. Why should Brad have made this connection and not her? It wasn't fair.

"However," Brad paused expectantly.

"What? However, what?"

"Well. Here's the thing. And I wanted to see what you thought before we did anything. You might not be up for it and if so, that's totally cool. I know you say you belong to me and I want that too, but I still believe you should have the power to say no, if something makes you uncomfortable."

Tess was seething with curiosity. "What! Tell me already!"

Brad laughed. "Patience is a virtue in a sub. Definitely one we need to cultivate in you." Finally he took pity on her. "Okay I'll tell you. James is very interested in you. He says you remind him of Olivia, with your fire and your passion, coupled with your innocence and naïveté."

Brad held up his hands, as if warding off a blow when Tess started to protest. Laughing again he said, "Hold on! Those are his words, not mine! Cool your jets, babe. Maybe he's right, you know. You are something of an innocent, for all your sluttish ways."

This time she lunged at him, but Brad was too quick for her, fending her off and then deftly pinning her arms underneath her. He lay across his captive, his long, hard body pressing against her soft, yielding one and he kissed her passionately until she went limp. When he pulled away, sitting up next to her, Tess reached up and begged him for another kiss.

"Don't you want to know what James has in mind for you, my darling?" That got her attention and Tess nodded, waiting, she hoped, patiently. Brad continued, "James wanted to know about what you and I have together. He wanted to understand what made our relationship truly a Dominant/submissive connection. I told him some of what we do. I told him you take a whipping well and obey my commands in a sexy and submissive way."

Tess flushed but she wasn't displeased. It was kind of embarrassing to know she had been talked about like that but also exciting. "He said he wondered if you'd be ready for the next step. He said he believed it was important for a submissive to flaunt her nature. Again, his words. George Hawkins wasn't the only one our Olivia was exposed to, you know.

"Though we've lost the diaries from later years, that didn't mean they stopped playing around! James regularly had men come into the office and Olivia was forced not only to display herself for these gentlemen, but eventually she was expected to 'service' them as well. She became his whore, Tess. And she reveled in it."

"Oh, my God," Tess whispered. It sounded so sordid. Yet, she knew that it hadn't been. She believed, based on how she'd watched Olivia blossom so quickly in just those few months, that she would have willingly gone each new step with her lover. That it had been a natural progression to first be exposed, then to submit to more and more, eventually involving the other men directly. It was the ultimate submission—a final loss of self.

Brad held Tess close. She could feel his tension, his excitement. "I want that. Tess, I want you to become my whore. My perfect, submissive whore. Do you understand what I'm asking?"

Tess felt that she did. It was a romantic request, in their own peculiar world of sadomasochism. She knew he didn't mean it in the traditional sense. He was asking for the ultimate proof of her devotion. For the ironic giving of herself to another, as a way to prove her very real and voluntary submission to him. Slowly she nodded, and asked, "And Mr. Stevenson—James. Where does he fit into all of this?" But she already knew the answer.

_*_

It had been Mr. Stevenson's idea to meet at the old downtown hotel where he and Olivia had met so many times in years gone by. They had agreed it would be exciting to meet there, possibly in the very room where Nana had submitted to her Master's endless loving tortures.

Brad had been somewhat surprised when Tess agreed to everything he'd suggested. He'd been prepared to negotiate, to allow her to wear more clothing, for example, to help maintain a reasonable comfort level. After all, though they'd been going deeper and deeper into their D/s roles, this would be their first public scene.

But she had agreed eagerly, excited to wear the sexy waist cincher she'd purchased to wear during their sessions, even agreeing to forego both panties and bra for the demonstration. She looked incredible, her hot little pussy splayed, the labia pooching alluringly between her legs.

She was secured to an aluminum frame, which Mr. Stevenson had brought with him. The ingenious device folded neatly into a one-by-three-foot container that looked like a case for a large musical instrument. When unfolded, it became a sturdy aluminum X-frame, with a pole across the top handy for securing a person up to six-feet tall. It was heavily weighted at the bottom so it wouldn't tip over, even if the bound person were to struggle. Mr. Stevenson told them he'd had it specially designed while in Italy some ten years before. The welder who had produced the item hadn't asked him what it was for and he hadn't volunteered.

Tess was tethered to the frame, her arms pulled taut overhead. She was blindfolded, the black satin an arresting contrast to her pale skin and brightly painted red lips. She looked so vulnerable and so impossibly sexy, spread eagle as she was, bound at the wrists and ankles.

She was wearing a wine-colored waist cincher that pulled in her already narrow waist and raised her luscious, bare breasts like an offering. Very high heels emphasized the fine curve of her calves, making her long legs look even longer. The eye was drawn up the leg to that perfect ass, full and round.

Brad and Mr. Stevenson sat together, both of them riveted to the beautiful, bound girl. They sipped their drinks, pretending, at least for Brad it was pretending, to be calm and collected. In fact he sported a raging hard-on and kept crossing and uncrossing his legs in an effort to hide it.

"She's lovely, Brad," Mr. Stevenson offered. "Sheer perfection. What an incredibly lucky man you are."

"She is," Brad agreed, unable to keep the pride out of his voice. He saw the slight smile curve Tess's lips. As nervous as he knew she was, he also knew she wanted this, maybe even more than he did.

"Show me what you brought," Mr. Stevenson said. Brad handed him the heavy flogger he now used regularly on his slave girl. Mr. Stevenson held it in two hands, admiring the heft of it. "It's weighted well," he commented. "Have you ever used anything else? A crop perhaps? Or the cane?"

Tess drew a small but audible breath. They both looked at her. "I see my words have an effect on your slave. She'll need to work on controlling her reactions. Most unbecoming in a slave girl, all that shuddering and sighing."

Slightly annoyed at the man's criticism, Brad responded, "We're still pretty new to the scene. The cane isn't something we've discussed yet. Tess and I are figuring things out together, one delicious step at a time."

"Of course." Mr. Stevenson nodded. "I didn't bring my cane today but I do have a nice little crop I brought with me. It's different from the flogger. A more contained sensation, if you will. Can be harder to take—gives your slave a chance to show her mettle more, if you see what I mean."

Slowly, Mr. Stevenson lumbered to his feet and walked toward the small table where he'd laid his briefcase. He took out a short black-handled riding crop with a loop of shiny black leather at its tip.

"Shall we give it a try? I can give you a brief demonstration and then you take over."

Brad moved over to Tess and touched her shoulder. She flinched at the unexpected contact. "Tess. Are you ready to try the crop? Remember, if you can't handle something, or it gets too intense, speak up. I not only don't want you silent, I want to know if something isn't right, okay?"

Tess nodded, taking a breath. Brad leaned down and kissed her lightly on the cheek. "I love you," he whispered. "Are you okay?"

"Yes," she whispered back.

Satisfied, Brad nodded toward Mr. Stevenson. He stepped toward Tess, moving just behind and to the side.

Slap! The little square of leather made contact with Tess's bottom and she jumped a little. Again it struck, this time on the left side. As the old gentleman struck her, he lectured on wrist position and angle. Then he stepped away, handing the crop to Brad.

"Still good, Tess?" Brad asked. Tess nodded, and let her head fall back, dark hair streaming behind her. God, she was lovely. Brad smacked her ass with the crop, enjoying the sound of the leather against her soft skin. He struck with more force, watching carefully for Tess's reaction. She was breathing hard through her nostrils, and jerking forward slightly with each strike. Brad liked the way it made her ass turn red.

Mr. Stevenson again stepped forward. "Let's see what she can take, Brad, shall we? If I may?"

Brad raised an eyebrow, surprised the old man wanted another shot. What the hell, he decided. Maybe he'd learn from an old pro. He handed the crop to Mr. Stevenson and stepped back to watch.

Leaning toward Tess, Mr. Stevenson commanded, "I want you to count, Tess. I'm going to crop you thirty times on each buttock and you will count. You don't have to count out loud, just keep track in your head so you know what to expect. This is going to hurt, but you know you need it."

"Oh," Tess said softly, and Brad knew Mr. Stevenson had struck a chord with his lover. She did need it. For both of them the D/s part of their relationship was no longer just a pleasure, it was a requirement. They both needed it to feel complete.

He began to crop her, carefully striking the same spot over and over until Tess began to squirm, trying in vain to twist away from the leather, her movements accompanied by breathy yelps of pain. Brad was counting in his head as well, and at twenty-six, Tess cried out, "No, no, I can't! Stop!"

Brad knew he would have stopped but Mr. Stevenson did not. "You can," Mr. Stevenson said implacably, giving her four more blows in rapid, stinging succession. With his other hand, Mr. Stevenson pressed against the red, tortured flesh until Tess stopped her jerking movements and stilled, leaning heavily against her wrist cuffs.

"Are you ready for the other side?" Mr. Stevenson asked politely.

If she said no, Brad was going to step in and end this. He would not have another man taking his sub girl faster than she was ready to go. But she was nodding and pulling herself upright.

"Speak, girl," Mr. Stevenson commanded. "Say what you mean."

"P-please, Sir," Tess stammered sweetly. "I'm ready for the other side."

"Good girl." Mr. Stevenson patted her ass and for a moment Brad wanted to strike him. He quickly got hold of himself, mentally chiding himself for being jealous of a man who was nearly eighty. Let the old guy have his fun. Tess was clearly enjoying herself and that was all that mattered.

Mr. Stevenson moved to the other side and again began the cropping, hitting the girl with precise strokes until she was again trying to twist away from the crop, crying out with each stinging slap of leather. But this time she didn't say stop, taking every last blow plus two extra the old sadist threw in for good measure.

"She did well, for her first time," he said, turning to Brad with a broad smile. "Of course, you'll need to train her not to wriggle around like that. It makes proper aim difficult."

"Had enough, baby?" he murmured as he removed Tess's blindfold and released the cuffs that held her tethered to the aluminum frame. She leaned heavily into his arms and he caught her, pulling her into an embrace before leading her on wobbly legs to the couch. Once they were seated, she buried her face in Brad's shoulder and nestled against him. He wrapped his arms around her and held her close.

Mr. Stevenson remarked, "She was magnificent, Brad. Like a wild mare, a glorious specimen of perfect femininity! I wasn't gentle, either. I took her further than

I ever took Olivia, as far as pain level. Because I sensed she could take it. She's a real masochist, Brad. In the most lovely and erotic sense. God, I envy you!"

Brad felt pride course through his veins. His girl had been brave and graceful, squirming notwithstanding. Brad's cock was so hard it hurt, pressing like iron against his jeans. He was glad when he realized Mr. Stevenson was packing to go. He easily broke down the aluminum restraining device with practiced ease.

He surprised Brad when he said, "Please accept this as a token of my appreciation for sharing your beautiful slave with me. I won't be needing it anymore. And now, with your permission, I will take my leave. Please enjoy the room, if you like. It's good until checkout tomorrow morning and I certainly have no need of it."

Mr. Stevenson smiled at them both as he moved toward the door. "Thank you for a most entertaining afternoon. It was like a bit of Olivia brought back to me, for just a moment. Treasure what you have, my dears. Life is so fleeting."

chapter 14

THEY WERE NOT to see Mr. Stevenson again. It was Tess's mother who mentioned she had seen his name in the obituary column. It was only six months after their adventure at the hotel. Life is fleeting, he had said then. Tess found herself wondering if he'd simply let go of life, now that both his wife and the woman he had loved in secret for forty years were no longer there to share it with him.

Tess had taken Brad home to meet her parents, who were properly impressed with his good looks, his charm and his promising career. Her father had joked that he could take good care of his little baby, and her mom, not quite joking, shot back that obviously Tess, a promising attorney in her own right, didn't need taking care of!

Brad and Tess had only smiled at one another. Their relationship was no longer a secret at work either, though of course no one there had any idea of role D/s played in their lives. No one at Reilly & Clark knew, for example, that Tess rarely wore underwear to work and when Brad buzzed her from his office, if possible she was to drop whatever she was working on and come to serve him in whatever capacity pleased him at the time.

There had been a few close calls, when Tess was on her knees under Brad's large desk, her lips wrapped around his cock when his secretary had returned early from lunch, entering his office after only a cursory knock.

Brad solved the problem by locking his office door when he didn't want to be interrupted. He explained to his secretary that he didn't like to be disturbed when he was working on an important case and that locking his door helped keep out the other attorneys who tended to wander in from time to time. If she didn't believe him, she had kept that to herself.

They each still worked ridiculous hours, as young attorneys often do, but spent every spare moment together. When at home, Tess was either naked or in one of her growing collections of waist cinchers. She loved the way they made her feel, as if Brad himself were gripping her waist, laying claim to her. They forced her to move with a certain grace and she'd taken to wearing them at work too, hidden beneath her conservative suits. She loved when Brad called her to his office and ordered her to his bathroom, where she was to strip down to her cincher and stockings and await his bidding.

Sometimes he would have her suck his cock. Or he might bend her over the sink and fuck her from behind, while watching her in the mirror. Other times he would just fondle her pussy until she was soaking wet and then send her back to work, on fire for him until the evening, when he'd stoke the flames all the higher.

Peter had moved out to buy his own place, and Tess had moved in, bringing her cat with her. The exercise room had been permanently converted to their playroom, complete with sturdy hooks in the ceiling for the chains and cuffs and various erotic torture devices that could be cleverly disguised as exercise equipment to the undiscerning eye.

As the months passed and the anniversary of their first date approached, Tess had never been happier. Secretly she reveled in the delicious irony of her life. The confidence she gained from achieving submissive grace at home was mirrored back in her professional life. Somehow by giving up control in her sexual life she had gained it in the workplace, making a name for herself much as Brad had done at the firm before her, with her ability to penetrate a case and win in court far more often than she lost. If only they knew what she did when she went home at night!

The couple fell into a routine that incorporated their D/s lifestyle seamlessly into their day. In addition to stealing moments in the office, as soon as they entered their car in the law firm's underground garage, each would undergo a subtle change.

It became habit for Tess to lift her skirt—she was never to wear pants—so that her bare ass made contact with the soft leather of Brad's luxury sedan. If she was wearing underwear that day—Brad permitted this on cold days—she would slip it off at once, offering the panties to Brad as a gesture of her submission to him.

He would take the little bit of silk and lace, hold it to his nose and inhale, his face a study in bliss. For some reason, this always made Tess blush, though it pleased her as well.

One evening when they got home after work and a quick bite to eat out, a discreet package wrapped in brown paper was waiting. It had Tess's name on it. As they sorted through the mail, Brad handed it to her.

"What's this? I don't remember ordering anything." Tess took the package, looking at the return address, which said only *JRH & Associates*. She glanced sharply at Brad, who was grinning at her. That was the name used for mailing by the online BDSM site where they ordered most of their goodies.

"Open it and see," Brad said.

Tess walked over to the sofa and sat down, pulling at the wrapping as she went. Inside were two pairs of some kind of clamps on sturdy silver chains. Tess was familiar with alligator clip nipple clamps, and indeed had been subjected to them, but these looked positively diabolical.

She held one out, examining it. "What the hell...? Tell me this isn't what I think it is?"

Brad's smile was slow, his eyes glittering. "And what do you think it is?"

"Some kind of clamps? But," she pushed at the sides of the oval metal ring, which opened the flat, rubber-tipped clamps, "these look dangerous. Ouch!"

"Not dangerous. But they aren't for beginners. They're called clover clamps." Brad sat beside her and lifted the second pair from the box. "The cool thing about these beauties is when you pull on them, instead of popping off, they actually get tighter."

Tess started in fascination as Brad demonstrated, open and shutting the spring mechanism. Involuntarily she reached for her breasts, covering the nipples already rising in anticipation of the clamps' pinch.

"Those are for my nipples? You think I can handle that?"

"I know you can, beautiful girl." Brad stroked her thigh, pushing her skirt up and moving his hand slowly toward her bare pussy.

"Spread your legs," he murmured and she shifted to obey, aware she was wet and swelling with desire at the thought of those wicked clamps compressing her sensitive nipples.

As his hand moved closer to her sex, a sudden dawning of horrified realization struck her. "Wait a minute," she said. "Why do we have two sets?"

Brad put his hand over her sex, cupping it. He slid a finger into her wetness and answered, "Why do you think, sub girl?"

Tess tried to close her legs. "No. No way. No."

Brad kept his hand between them, still cupped firmly over her pussy. "You're telling me no? My obedient little sub girl is saying no to her Master?" He was still smiling but Tess could hear the steel beneath his words.

Her heart had begun to flutter. "Well, I mean, come on, Brad. You can't be thinking..."

"Of clamping your labia? Of course I can. Why ever not? You would look incredibly hot like that, Tess. And it would put you an excellent submissive headspace, I'm sure of it."

"Oh, Brad," Tess breathed. Despite her trepidation, her clit was now throbbing, her sex swelling like a parched flower turning toward rain. She already knew with her body that she wanted to feel the bite of those clamps on her nipples and pussy, but still her mouth uttered one last protest.

"What if I can't do it? What if it hurts too much?"

Brad pulled her gently into his arms. Whispering into her hair, he said, "My love, you can do whatever I tell you to do. Haven't you proved that over and over? Without fear there is no courage—we've learned that together. Sometimes it takes courage to submit. But the rewards are invariably worth it, don't you agree? Have I steered you wrong yet?"

She had to admit that he had not. Each new step on her submissive journey had brought her closer to a deep inner peace that left her breathless with joy.

"Forgive me, Sir. I forgot myself," she said in a low voice.

Brad stood, still holding one set of the clover clamps. He held out his hand and Tess took it, allowing him to help her stand. She clutched the second pair of clamps.

Slowly Brad spun her around so he was pressing his front against her back. He unbuttoned and slipped off her suit jacket, leaving the silk camisole underneath in place.

He pushed a strap down, licking along the curve of her neck, sending shivers through her body. With one large hand, he reached around her, wrapping his fingers around her throat. As always, this produced a tremor of submissive desire in Tess.

"Who do you belong to?" he whispered into her ear.

"You, my love," she murmured back, trying to twist around to kiss him. But he held her still, increasing the pressure at her throat just slightly, making her catch her breath.

He let her go, turning her to face him. "Tonight you will prove it once again. Give me the clamps." He held out his hand and Tess dropped the second pair with a clank onto the first. "Would you like to shower before we play?"

"Yes, please."

Brad nodded. "Okay. Present yourself when you're ready. I'll go open us a bottle of wine."

Tess hurried to the bathroom, now deeply excited. Brad liked her to keep her labia completely shaved and smooth, while leaving a neat little patch on the top. She loved the feel of her smooth lips and often touched herself during the day at her desk, enjoying the silky soft skin, sometimes sneaking a finger inside of herself and occasionally even rubbing herself to orgasm.

She stood in the steamy shower soaping up her pussy to get what little stubble might have accumulated since her early morning shower nice and soft for shaving. She squirted some baby oil onto her fingers and rubbed it into the folds. Taking a fresh razor, she pulled it up along the labia until they were baby-smooth.

She toweled off quickly, coming into the bedroom to find her darling man waiting with crisp white wine in two long-stemmed wineglasses. He held out a glass for her and she sipped the delicious chardonnay.

She studied the handsome lines of Brad's face as she drank her wine. How she loved this man who had become such an important part of her world. Who could possibly understand the rich and complex tapestry of their relationship now? Lovers and equal partners, but with a consensual exchange of power that now allowed Brad to say, "I'm going to put the clamps on your nipples first. Offer your breasts to me."

Tess set her glass down on the nightstand and lifted a breast in each hand. The nipples were already erect, eagerly perking toward Brad. He gripped one between his thumb and index finger, pulling it taut. With the other hand, he pressed the sides of the oval spring mechanism so the flat, rubber-tipped clamps opened. Positioning her nipple at the opening, he let the spring close and Tess yelped.

"You okay?" he asked, tugging gently at the clamp, which held firm.

Tess blew out a breath through pursed lips. "Yes. It's very tight, but yes. I can handle it." As it always did, the pain tripping along her nerve endings was blending with the searing ache of desire deep inside her. Her pussy was throbbing and her other nipple was tingling in anticipation.

He clamped the second nipple and again Tess offered the long, slow hiss of breath through pursed lips as she worked through the pain. She could feel herself ascending to that altered state where she felt she would do anything for her man.

Gently Brad pushed her back so she lay flat against the bed, the silver chain resting against her chest between her breasts. She closed her eyes as Brad smoothed his hands down her body. He pushed her thighs apart and stroked her spread labia, already wet with desire and anticipation.

"You can do this, Tess. I know you can. You were born for this."

Tess opened her eyes and nodded slowly. He was right. She was born for this. She watched as he opened one of the clamps, He tugged at her right outer lip, pulling it taut. He held the open clamp, and, positioning it on either side of the lip, he let it close.

"Ah, Jesus," Tess cried. Her hands curled into fists and she began to pant.

"Shh, shh," Brad soothed. "It's okay. You're fine." While he spoke, he pulled at and secured the second lip, drawing another cry from Tess.

"Slow your breathing. You're doing great. Shh, breathe deep. Focus, Tess. You can do this. Breathe through it." He stroked her thighs and bent down to kiss her cheek. The pain was in fact lessening as her nipples and labia numbed somewhat to it. It still hurt, make no mistake, but she found she could tolerate it.

"Want to see?" Brad said.

Tess nodded, accepting his hand as he helped her to rise from the bed. The chains between her breasts and legs swayed as she walked awkwardly toward the full-length mirror mounted on the back of the bathroom door.

"Oh," she said, taking in the sight of her blood-engorged nipples compressed between the clamps, the large silver ovals hanging beneath them and the U of the chain between them. But what really riveted her attention were the clamps at her sex. She stared in fascination at how they separated and stretched her labia, the silver chain dangling beneath them.

Brad came to stand behind her. Wrapping his arms around her, he brought one hand down between her legs. This caused the chain to sway, which added pressure on her tortured labia. Tess gasped with pain that rapidly changed to pleasure when Brad began to finger her very wet cunt, rubbing and moving between the clamps over her hard clit and into her burning tunnel.

As he finger-fucked her, he commanded, "Look, Tess. Look in the mirror. Look at that gorgeous, sexy woman in the mirror." She forced her eyes open, seeing herself through his eyes, a sexy, naked woman with clamped nipples and pussy, her lips slack with lust, her hair wild about her face.

Her eyes fluttered shut as he brought her quickly to the edge of an intense climax. "Please, Sir," she breathed. "May I...?"

"Yes." He pushed three fingers inside her, moving them in such a way she began to buck and jerk against him, completely out of control. The swaying chains caused the clamps to tighten as she moved, adding pain to the heightening pleasure, sweeping her completely into a blinding, searing orgasm.

Tess fell back heavily against her lover, who held her easily, his fingers still buried inside her. Her legs gave way and she sagged against him, her heart thumping in her ears, her body limp.

Brad lifted and carried her to the bed, laying her gently down. "I'm going to take them off, Tess. Just a moment of pain and then it'll be over." He released the nipple clamps first and Tess cried out, her hands flying to her tortured nipples as the blood flow rushed back into the tender buds.

When he unclipped her labia, Tess screamed, the pain like a stinging rain of bee stings. She tried to clamp her legs together but Brad held them apart. Her cries soon turned to moans when Brad soothed the sting with his tongue, licking away the pain until she nearly passed out from pleasure.

_*_

Later in the week Tess and Brad sat at the dinner table, finishing the pasta and shrimp salad they'd made together. Brad took a long drink of his merlot. "So, you're sure about this, Tess?"

Tess bit her lower lip. "Yes. I think."

Brad laughed. "Then we'll wait a while longer. There's no hurry, love. This is for you. It has to be something you're *sure* you want."

Tess nodded. She did want it, but she was afraid. When Brad had first put the idea out there several months before, she'd categorically refused. No way in hell was someone going to put a needle through her labia! Just the thought made her cringe. She was terrified of needles. Just doing blood work for her annual physical made her faint.

Brad had let it go, telling her that while he liked the idea of a piece of jewelry at her pussy, something secret only the two of them would know about, he only wanted it if and when she did.

Wanting to please her lover, and questioning her own submissiveness for refusing him point blank, Tess began to research the idea with more seriousness, though she didn't mention this to Brad and nor did he bring up the subject again.

One night while lying in bed, she mentioned she'd been looking around the Internet, reading up on the matter and that maybe it wouldn't be so terrible. "It doesn't hurt nearly as much as piercing your nipple or belly button," she told him. "And if I didn't look while it was being done, I think I'd be okay."

"That's great, Tess. But we're not going to do it. Not unless it's something you want."

"Well. Okay." She was silent a while. "It is kind of sexy though. The pictures. I might like that. You know, something pretty. Something special. Something that signifies your sensual ownership of me."

"I would like that." Brad leaned over and kissed her nose. "Very much. But we're not doing it," he repeated. "Not unless you really want it. I don't want you doing it just for me."

As the days turned into weeks, the idea had taken hold of Tess and wouldn't let go. She did want it, damn it, so why did Brad keep saying no? She knew why. It was because she equivocated. She never said, "I want this, Brad." She always added, "I think," or made it clear through body language and tone of voice that she wasn't really ready. Would she ever be really ready to have a sharp needle pierce her flesh?

She recalled the scene in Charlotte's Awakening, one which had both fascinated and horrified her when she'd first read it. When Brad had first brought up the idea of the piercing, she'd found the passage again.

"It's not enough to mark you with the whip. It's not enough that you wear my chains at your throat, your waist, your ankles. I want you to wear my chains at your sex."

Charlotte kept her head down, eyes cast properly on the floor. She was still as a statue, the only evidence that she had even heard her Master a slight movement of her bare shoulders. Sir Jonathan pulled her up, forcing her to stand in front of him, her crimson velvet gown crushed as he pulled her to him.

"I want it to be permanent, Charlotte. I'm going to pierce your flesh and lock your sex with these chains." He held up a bracelet of fine gold. Its clasp on one end came to a very sharp point. The other end was a spring mechanism which, once engaged, would not open again.

As Charlotte paled, Sir Jonathan went on, "Tonight when I come for you, I want you naked in the bath. I will pierce your labia and insert this lovely jewelry. Just one more proof that you belong completely and utterly to me."

He caught her as she swayed and fainted into his arms. Her display, while charming, would gain her no pity and certainly no reprieve.

Tess shivered even though she knew the words were fiction. The man was an ass! Brad would never "inform" her about what he would do to her. Though she adored submitting to him, the exchange of power was always and completely voluntary.

Sitting now at the dinner table with her dominant lover, Tess wondered what it would be like to be so completely enslaved, as Charlotte had been in the novel. Did such relationships really exist? Could there possibly be a foundation of love and trust when one partner truly had no choice in the matter?

Yes, she was scared to be pierced. But he wanted it. Wasn't that enough? No. She had to want it too. Tess banged her fist on the table, making their wine glasses rattle. "I *do* want it. I'm certain, Brad. I do want it."

Brad looked at her, tilting his head in that appraising way he had. "I believe you," he said finally. Pushing back from the chair, he added, "I'll be right back. I have to get something."

He returned a moment later, holding out a small ring box covered in dark blue velvet. "You already had it? But what if...?"

"What if you never wanted it? Then it would have just sat forever in the drawer. But I had a feeling..." He grinned and Tess grinned back. She took the offered box and opened it. Inside was a solid gold hoop shaped like a horseshoe, with a little red jewel on either end. They looked like garnets or rubies.

Brad looked expectantly at her. "Do you like it? It's removable, see?" He lifted the little ring from where it nestled in velvet, untwisting one of the gems to show Tess it wouldn't be permanent. "That way, if you don't like it or it bothers you, you can take it off. Just like earrings."

"Only sexier," Tess said, as Brad dropped the beautiful piece of jewelry into her palm.

"Much," Brad agreed.

*

Tess was glad the body piercing artist Brad had chosen was a woman. Her name was Sandra, and according to Brad she had an excellent reputation for doing fast, painless work.

The place was called The Golden Butterfly. On the wall there hung a framed photograph of a woman's pussy, shaved and tattooed to look like a butterfly, the bulk of the design on the mons above the folds. The inner labia were its lower wings, and they and the clit hood were decorated with numerous rings. The effect was stunning, if a little frightening, and Tess couldn't stop staring at the picture.

"You like it?"

"It's amazing," Tess breathed.

"Thanks. My boyfriend did the tattoo art, I did the rings. I used to call this place the 'Rings of Desire' but when we did that one, I knew I had to change it." Sandra was swabbing the area as she spoke, behaving in such a matter-of-fact manner that Tess found herself calming down.

She had gulped several ounces of brandy before they left the house. Courage in a bottle, her dad would call it, but she was still extremely nervous.

Sandra and Brad conferred a moment and then Sandra placed a little dot with a marker where Brad indicated that he wanted the piercing. They both seemed so calm and relaxed that Tess felt almost foolish being so nervous.

I wanted this, she reminded herself over and over. *I want this.*

Sandra took out a menacing-looking item. "This is just a clamp," she explained. "It's used to hold the skin taut. That way you only pierce the minimum amount of tissue, resulting in the minimum amount of pain. Now this—" she swabbed a gel onto the labia, rendering it almost numb, "—is a local anesthetic. You'll hardly feel anything after this."

Sandra took the ring from its box. "This is lovely. Where did you get it?"

"I had it especially made, by Dream Rings, online. It turned out even better than I'd expected." Brad beamed.

Tess winced when Sandra unwrapped a fresh piercing needle. "Don't look," Brad said. "It'll all be over in a second." Easy for him to say. He wasn't the one with his legs spread wide, waiting for a very sharp needle to pierce his flesh.

"That's right," Sandra affirmed. "It probably hurt worse to pierce your ears than this will. Just stay very still. Close your eyes and relax. I'm going to count to three and you just take nice, deep breaths." She stroked Tess's hair, her touch soothing.

"One, two, *three*." On three she slipped the needle through the delicate labile fold. Tess drew in a sharp breath but managed to stay still. The only betrayal of her nerves were her hands, knuckles white as she clenched the soft padded arms of the chair.

Though Tess couldn't see, she knew what was happening, based on her research. Once the piercing needle was withdrawn, it left a hollow plastic catheter still sticking through the skin. Sandra would insert the stem of the ring into the catheter and then remove the plastic, leaving the jewelry in place. Sandra screwed the little gem onto the threaded stud and the operation was complete. The whole procedure took less than a minute.

"Want to see?" Sandra held a large hand mirror up to Tess, who still had her eyes squeezed tight.

She opened them in surprise. "You mean it's done already?" She broke into a broad grin, and drew in a deep breath of relief. Taking the mirror, she positioned it to see her pussy. The little ring looked exotic, beautiful and sexy as hell. Tess smiled up at Brad as he bent down to kiss her.

_*_

As Tess soaked in a hot bath, she mused about the past year that had brought them to this moment. She looked down at the sparkling one-carat diamond on her finger, flanked by small, perfect blue sapphires. Brad had asked her to marry him and she had eagerly accepted, thinking of the old-fashioned vows in which the wife promised to honor and obey her husband and how that would fit into their secret, wonderful lifestyle.

She slipped a hand between her legs, fingering the little golden and ruby jewel tucked into the folds of her pussy. She rubbed idly for a moment, savoring the touch, aware she mustn't come. She was never to masturbate without Brad's express permission. Rather than feeling constricted by this command, she thrilled to it, as she did all of his rules and rituals. She had never felt more alive and more validated than she did as Brad's sexual submissive.

Who knew if she would ever have traveled this path, if it hadn't been for Nana and those secret diaries? Would she have ever gotten in touch with her own submissive feelings if not for reading the searing words, written so long ago, with passion and love? Would she have found a safe way to share her fledgling feelings with Brad? Or would they both have harbored their own secret longings, their own secret needs, never daring to share what had become a centerpiece of their relationship?

She would never know, but she did know that she was deeply grateful for having discovered and read the diaries. And she felt closer to her grandmother, closer even than when she had been alive. Though at first she had been afraid it would ruin her idea of her dear old Nana, now she appreciated that a woman could be a vibrant sexual being and still be a good mother and grandmother.

How lonely for Olivia, not to have been able to share her own orientation with her husband. For Tess had come to believe her submissive nature was an orientation, like being left-handed or gay. Still, Olivia had been able to discover and share it with her long-time lover, Mr. Stevenson. How funny that she called him that all through the journals, despite their obvious change from boss and secretary to lovers. Still, they had had a much longer relationship than what was recorded in those little notebooks, and perhaps over time she had come to call him James.

Tess soaked a while longer in the fragrant water, soft with bath oils. Soon she would get out and dry herself, and present herself to her lover, kneeling naked in their playroom, with her forehead on the carpet, her legs spread, her ass and pussy offered for whatever use amused her Master.

Tess felt herself ascending into that wonderful submissive state of mind where she was at once completely at peace, but with a mantle of fiery passion dropped down onto her shoulders. It was a delicious and potent dichotomy that never lost its power.

She climbed out of the tub and wrapped a large towel around her body. She was surprised to see Brad lying on the bed when she entered. She had expected him to be in their study, finishing some work while he waited for her to prepare herself for him.

He was naked, his cock erect over his flat, strong stomach. He smiled a lazy, seductive smile. "Come here, sexy girl," he said, holding out his arms. Tess dropped her towel and joined him on the bed, reveling in his strong arms as they wrapped around her.

Brad drew a finger down her cheek, moving it over her lips so they parted. She sucked on the finger and he pressed it back, deep into her mouth, like a cock. She felt wanton, sexual, beautiful.

All her life, Tess had been driven, always rushing on to the next big thing. Until she'd met Brad, until she'd found this new and deeply satisfying lifestyle, she'd believed it was just her nature to press forward, head down, never stopping to take in the moment.

Brad pulled his finger away and looked at Tess, the love in his eyes so bright Tess actually caught her breath.

"I belong to you," she whispered.

"We belong to each other," he answered.

Made in the USA